PENGUIN BOOKS

A SAVAGE PLACE

Robert B. Parker was born in 1932 and has a Ph.D. from Boston University. He has been Professor of English at Northeastern University, Massachusetts, USA, teaching courses in American literature, and has written several serious text books, including *The Personal Response to Literature*. He has written ten other novels featuring his wry Boston private detective, Spenser; of these, Penguin publish *The Godwulf Manuscript*, *God Save the Child*, *Mortal Stakes*, *Promised Land*, *The Judas Goat*, *Early Autumn* and *Valediction*. *Promised Land* won the Edgar Allan Poe Award in the USA for the best mystery novel of 1976.

Robert Parker has also written a non-Spenser novel, *Wilderness*. An enthusiastic sportsman, he is the author of *Sports Illustrated Weights Training*. He lives north of Boston with his wife and their two sons and his hobbies include jogging and tennis.

D0620514

A SAVAGE PLACE

PLACE

Robert B. Parker

PENGUIN BOOKS

Penguin Books Ltd, Harmondsworth, Middlesex, England
Viking Penguin Inc., 40 West 23rd Street, New York, New York 10010, U.S.A.
Penguin Books Australia Ltd, Ringwood, Victoria, Australia
Penguin Books Canada Ltd, 2801 John Street, Markham, Ontario, Canada L3R 1B4
Penguin Books (N.Z.) Ltd, 182–190 Wairau Road, Auckland 10, New Zealand

First published in the U.S.A. by Delacorte Press 1981
First published in Great Britain by Judy Piatkus (Publishers) Ltd 1982
Published in Penguin Books 1985

Made and printed in Great Britain by
Richard Clay (The Chaucer Press) Ltd,
Bungay, Suffolk
Set in Linotype Baskerville

And there were gardens bright with sinuous rills,
Where blossomed many an incense-bearing tree;
And here were forests ancient as the hills,
Enfolding sunny spots of greenery.
But oh! that deep romantic chasm which slanted
Down the green hill athwart a cedarn cover!
A savage place! as holy and enchanted
As e'er beneath a waning moon was haunted
By woman wailing for her demon-lover!

SAMUEL TAYLOR COLERIDGE, "Kubla Khan"

Chapter 1

I WAS SITTING in my office above the bank with my tie loose and my feet up, reading a book called *Play of Double Senses: Spenser's Faerie Queene*. Susan Silverman had given it to me, claiming it was my biography. But it wasn't. It turned out to be about the sixteenth-century English poet who spelled his name like mine. The guy that wrote it had become the president of Yale, and I thought maybe if I read it, I could become Allan Pinkerton.

I was just starting the chapter titled "Pageant, Show, and Verse" when the phone rang. I picked it up and said in as deep a voice as I could, "Allan Pinkerton, here."

At the other end a voice I remembered said, "Mr. Spenser, please."

I said in my Pinkerton voice, "One moment, please," and then in my normal voice, "Hello."

The voice on the phone said, "Spenser, do you expect to deceive anyone with that nonsense?"

I said, "You want to hear me do Richard Nixon?"

"No, I do not. I haven't time. Spenser, this is Rachel Wallace. I assume you recall me."

"Often," I said.

"Well, I have some work for you."

"Let me check my schedule," I said.

She laughed briefly. "Your sense of humor is much too complete for you to be busy."

"Are you suggesting I offend people?"

"Yes. Myself included, upon occasion."

"Only upon occasion?"

"Yes."

"What would you like done?"

"There's a young woman in California who is in trouble. She needs the kind of help that you are able to offer."

"Where in California?"

"Los Angeles. She has uncovered what appears to be a large scandal in the motion picture industry and she fears that her life may become endangered."

"And you'd like me to go out and look after her?"

"Yes."

"I didn't do all that well with you."

"I think you did. I recommended you to this woman."

"She's a friend?"

"No, I met her only once. She's a television reporter and she interviewed me on the last leg of a book tour. I told her about our adventures. Later on she contacted me through my publisher and requested your name."

"You must have spoken well of me."

"I told the truth. You are strong and brave and resourceful. I told her that. I told her also that our politics were miles apart."

"Politics is too abstract for me," I said. "I don't have any."

"Perhaps you don't. I told her if you were committed, you would never give up and that, politics aside, you were quite intelligent."

"Intelligent?"

"Yes."

"I'm reading a book by the president of Yale," I said.

"Good for you. Will you help the young woman in California?"

"I need more details."

"She will supply them. I told her I'd call and clear the way, so to speak."

"When will I hear from her?"

"This afternoon. Shortly after I hang up."

"What's her name?"

"Candy Sloan. Will you do it?"

"Probably."

"Good. Give my love to Susan."

"Okay."

"Perhaps next time I'm in Boston, I can buy you lunch."

"Yes," I said. "Call me."

"I shall. Good-bye, Spenser."

"Good-bye."

I hung up the phone and stood and stared out the window. It was June. Below, at the corner of Berkley and Boylston, good-looking women in summer dresses crossed at the light. A lot of men wore seersucker jackets. I didn't. Susan said I wasn't the type. I asked her what type I was. She said leather vest, no shirt. I think she was kidding. It was June, seventy-two degrees, clear. The murder count in the city was down ten percent from last year, and I was willing to bet that somewhere someone was hugging the bejeepers out of something.

I looked at my watch. Four thirty. Susan was taking another summer course at Harvard, and I was supposed to pick her up at five. In L.A. that was barely past lunchtime. They were probably still sipping Perrier at Ma Maison.

Across Berkley Street the young dark-haired art director in the ad agency looked out the window and waved at me. I shot at her with my forefinger and she smiled. I smiled back. Enigmatic. Byronic. Once you have found her, never let her go. The phone rang. I said hello.

"Mr. Spenser?"

"Yes."

"This is Candy Sloan."

"Rachel Wallace spoke of you," I said.

"Oh, good. Then you know the situation."

"Only very generally," I said. "Rachel said you'd give me details."

"Oh, God. Over the phone? I hate to talk about it."

"How about I make up a set of circumstances and you tell me if I'm getting hot or cold?"

"Excuse me? Oh, you're being ironic. Rachel warned me that you would be."

"Ironic," I said.

"Well, of course you'll need to know things. I can give you details when you get out here, but essentially the situation is this. I'm a reporter for KNBS-TV, here in Los Angeles. We're doing an investigative series on labor racketeering in the film business, and I came across pretty solid evidence that production companies were paying off labor-union figures to ensure a trouble-free shooting schedule."

I said, "Um-hmm."

"When we started digging a little deeper, I got a threatening phone call and recently, when I've gotten off work, the same car, a maroon Pontiac Firebird with mag wheels, has followed me home."

"What was your pretty solid evidence?"

"It's followed me three nights in a row."

"No, I mean of payola in the movies?"

"Oh. Eyewitness."

"And what deeper digging did you do?"

"We began questioning other people in the business."

"Any documentary evidence?"

"Like checks, photographs, that sort of thing?"

"Yes. Stuff that couldn't be threatened or bought off."

"Not yet."

I had the phone tucked into the hollow of my shoulder and my hands in my hip pockets. While I talked, I looked out the window.

I said, "Um-hmm."

"So," Candy Sloan said, "the station has agreed to hire someone to help me with this. To act as a bodyguard and help with the investigation."

"Why not someone out there?" I took my left hand out of my pocket and looked at my watch. Four forty-six. I was going to be late for Susan if I didn't close this off.

"We couldn't be sure they would be reliable, and by coincidence, I had recently interviewed Rachel Wallace, and she spoke at length about her kidnapping and how you found her."

"She mention how I lost her in the first place?"

"She said that was her fault."

"Mmm."

"Will you come out here?"

"Two hundred dollars a day and expenses."

"That will be fine. The station will pay."

"And you gotta promise to show me a movie star."

"Anyone special?"

"Dale Evans."

There was silence on the other end.

"Or whoever you can find," I said. "It doesn't have to be Dale. Mala Powers would be good."

"I'll do what I can," she said. "Are you really this goofy all the time?" There was a giggle at the edge of her voice.

"Goofy?" I said. "When I meet Mala Powers, I'm going to tell her you said that."

"All right," she said. "When will you arrive? I'll meet you at the airport."

"I'll take the noon flight on American. Gets in at four."

"You've been to Los Angeles before?"

"Yes."

"Do you like it?"

"I think so," I said. "It makes me smile a lot."

"Good," she said. "Fly first class. The station won't blink. I'll page you when your flight arrives."

I looked at my watch. Ten of five. If the traffic was okay, I might still make it on time. "Okay," I said. "See you tomorrow."

"Good. Is there anything about you that would make you easy to recognize? Rachel told me you were big."

"Yeah. I look just like Cary Grant would have if he'd been hit often in the nose."

She giggled again. It was a nice sound. I liked it. She didn't sound too awful scared, and I kind of like that too.

"See you tomorrow," she said.

"Yes," I said. And hung up.

Chapter 2

CANDY SLOAN met me by the car rentals next to the baggage pickup at the L.A. airport. She had hair the color of jonquils and skin the color of honey and eyes the color of cornflowers. The good coloring was not wasted on the rest of her.

She said, "Is your name Spenser?"

I said yes.

She said, "I wasn't sure. I thought it might be Cary Grant."

"After a bad flight," I said.

She smiled. "I'm Candy Sloan," she said.

"Good," I said. "Show me a movie star."

"Let's get your luggage first," she said and went through the doors toward the carousels.

I watched her for a moment. She was wearing skin-tight jeans with someone's name on the butt and spiked heels. She had that rolling, arm-swinging walk that spike heels produce in agile women, and even here in Tinsel Town she turned a lot of heads. The top half (when I got to it) was covered with a scarlet blouse worn open over a lavender T-shirt. Around her neck were many gold chains. Her earrings were gold, and she wore several gold rings.

She looked back at me and smiled again. "Coming?"

I nodded and trailed after her. She was tall; with her spiked heels, nearly as tall as I was. Her hair was long and smooth, touching her shoulders. The first pieces of luggage were beginning to circle the carousel as we got to it. Mine was not yet out.

"Good flight?" she asked.

"First class is very pleasant," I said. "There was a former governor up there with me."

"How exciting for you."

"Well, he's no Tom Conway, you know?"

"Or Mala Powers," she said.

When she smiled, two lines deepened on either side of her mouth. Once you saw them, you realized they were always there. They were faint except when she smiled. Her nose was nice and straight and her eyebrows were darker than her hair. So were her eyelashes, which were long. There were several explanations for the dark hair–light hair contrast. I was speculating about them when my suitcase showed up. I snagged it and nodded toward the door.

She asked, "One suitcase?"

"Yep."

"My God, how do you travel with one suitcase?"

"It's mostly full of ammunition," I said. "If I'm not working, I can get by with a gym bag."

Outside the heat was solid. On a crosswalk in a tow zone reserved for authorized vehicles only was a Ford Fairlane station wagon with a whip antenna and an emblem on the side that read KNBS: THE SOUND OF THE GOLDEN WEST. Underneath that it said in smaller letters LIVE ACTION NEWS. A young airport cop with blond hair and a bushy blond mustache was leaning on the near front fender, his legs crossed, his arms folded over his chest. When he saw Candy Sloan, he stepped around and opened the door on the driver's side for her. She smiled at him and said, "Thank you."

He said, "Anytime, Miss Sloan," and carefully closed the door for her.

I opened the rear door, put my suitcase on the rear

seat, closed the door, opened the front door, and got in beside Miss Sloan. The cop ignored me. When I got my door closed, he blew a sharp whistle, held up a commanding hand, and stopped traffic while Miss Sloan pulled out of the tow zone and drove away.

"I suspect that man of sexism," I said.

"Really?"

"Yes. If I'd parked there, he'd have shot me."

"Oh, I don't think so, really," she said. "News people get a break, and they should." She turned the air conditioning up. I was glad.

"Mmm."

"Want the scenic route or the expressway?"

"Where we going?"

"The Beverly Hills was booked and so was the Beverly Wilshire. But I got a nice room at the Beverly Hillcrest. It's where the station always puts people. It's on the south edge of Beverly Hills. Beverwil Drive at Pico."

"Up back of the Beverly Wilshire about six blocks," I said.

"Yes, that's right. You have been here before."

I sucked down my upper lip and said, "I've been everywhere before, sweetheart."

She giggled. "Bogie?" she asked.

I said, "That's the way it is, kid."

She said, "That's awful."

I said, "You should hear my Allan Pinkerton impression."

She shook her head. "Freeway or scenic," she said.

"Why not go up Sepulveda for a while," I said.

The landscape was sere and hostile, naked-looking under the oppressive sun. I always felt a little exposed in Southern California.

I said, "Do you see my function as predominantly protective or predominantly investigative?"

"Protective, I think. I'm a good investigator. I need

someone to keep people from inhibiting the investigation."

"Okay," I said. "If I see a purloined letter lying about, I assume you won't mind if I mention it."

"I'd be grateful," she said. "But you wanted to know the priorities."

"Yes, I did."

"You're not going to go into a male funk on me, are you?" she said.

"It's the only funk I'm capable of," I said.

"I mean, you're not hung up about me saying I'm probably as good an investigator as you are?"

"No."

"I'm good at my job," she said. "Everyone thinks you get by on TV by wiggling your ass off-camera and saying everything with a bright smile on-camera."

"And," I said.

"And some of that is true, but I'm a damn good reporter."

"And the ass?"

She looked at me with the two lines deepening. "I wiggle that," she said, "when I want to. And where."

"Let me know the next time," I said. "I'll want to watch."

Again she smiled. I realized she could make that smile with the consonant eye-sparkle whenever she wished. Along with it went a giggle this time. That, too, I realized, was something she could do or not when she wished.

We turned on to Pico, heading east. "The thing is," Candy said, "that you need to understand that I'm in charge of the investigation. It's my story. I want to play it out."

"Sure," I said.

"That doesn't bother you?"

"No."

"Do you think I'm too aggressive and pushy?"

"Yeah. You don't need to be. But you don't know that. No harm in it."

"I'm in a tough business," she said. "I've learned to be tough. It frightens some men."

"I'll be okay," I said.

"Good," she said. "Is there anything you're dying to get off your chest?"

"Well," I said. "While it is true that I can leap tall buildings at a single bound, and while, in fact, I am more powerful than a locomotive, it is not true that I am faster than a speeding bullet. If I'm going to protect you, we have to weigh risk and gain quite often."

She nodded. "It's disappointing though," she said.

"What is?"

"That you're not faster than a speeding bullet."

"Think how I feel," I said.

We swung into the entrance of the Beverly Hillcrest. "Take a shower," she said. "Have a drink. Dinner in the room. Get rid of jet lag. Have a night's rest. I'll pick you up at eight thirty tomorrow morning, and you start working."

"You'll be okay tonight," I said.

"I was all right last night."

I got out. A servant took my suitcase. Everyone else watched Candy Sloan drive away. The folks at the Hillcrest didn't seem too much more laid-back than I was.

Chapter 3

IF YOU LOOKED straight out from the small balcony outside my room at the Beverly Hillcrest, you could see the Hollywood Hills and the sign that said HOLLYWOOD, and the sparse high-rises along Sunset and Hollywood boulevards. If you looked down, you could see the parking lot and the side entrance to the hotel. In between the parking lot and the hills you could survey the immaculate, peculiar stillness of Beverly Hills.

I drank coffee and ate a slice of fresh pineapple and some whole wheat toast. It was seven in the morning. I had neglected to bring my silk robe with the velvet lapels and was forced to lounge on the balcony shirtless, wearing a pair of blue shorts and no shoes. My feet were pale and eastern-looking. Actually so was my chest. Humiliating. I finished breakfast. By seven fifteen I had on my running shoes and a beige T-shirt with the sleeves cut off, and I was heading north on Beverly Drive at an easy jog. The T-shirt had one of those computer-printout pictures of Susan on it. We'd thought it was funny in a shopping mall last December. I figured the beige color would look like a tan from a distance.

The streets were spotless and empty of foot traffic. The houses were predominantly Spanish-Tudor-Colonial-Modern, showing the influences of Christopher Wren, Frank Lloyd Wright, and Walter Disney. Across

Wilshire I was into the heart of sleekness. Three short blocks at a faster pace and it was behind me. I was across Santa Monica Boulevard and back in residential elegance.

I ran up Beverly to the little park in front of the Beverly Hills Hotel on Sunset, turned around, and ran back down Rodeo Drive. Huge palms with pine-appley bark lined the streets. Back across both Santa Monicas. (Was there anywhere else, I thought, that had two streets running side by side with the same name? No, I thought. There wasn't.) Rodeo Drive was even more epically chic than Beverly Drive. The names of internationally known hairdressers graced the windows of small buildings elegantly crafted of fake stone and make-believe stucco. People didn't seem to get up early here. I was still nearly alone, and the shops were mostly closed. If I were an international hairdo superstar, I'd probably sleep in myself. I wondered if they all talked funny, or just the ones I'd seen on television. Maybe you have to talk that way or when you're in New York, you can't get into Studio 54.

I arrived back at the hotel at eight with a pretty good sweat worked up. At eight thirty I had showered the sweat off, shaved, and put on my best warm-weather wardrobe. Summer-weight blue blazer, gray slacks, yellow Oxford shirt from Brooks Brothers, button-down collar worn without a tie, top two buttons open so I would look real Coast. In the breast pocket of the blazer I had a yellow silk show handkerchief; on the feet, cordovan loafers; on the right hip, a gun. I slipped into a pair of sunglasses I'd bought once in the Fairmont Hotel in Dallas. Then I checked the mirror. Should I unbutton the shirt two more buttons and wear a bullet around my neck on a gold chain? Too pushy. They might think I was an agent.

The phone rang. I answered. A man's voice said, "Mr. Spenser?"

"Yes."

"My name's Rafferty. I'm in the lobby. Candy Sloan asked me to come by and get you. She's been hurt and wants to see you."

"I'll be right down," I said.

"I'm driving a yellow Mazda RX7. I'll be right outside the door."

I went down the seven flights rather than wait for the elevator.

Rafferty was where he said he'd be. He was standing on the driver's side with the door partially open, one foot in the car.

I got into the Mazda, and he slipped into his side, snapped it into gear, spun the car around in the driveway, and rammed it out of the driveway and onto Beverly Drive at a considerable rate.

"What happened?" I said.

"She got beat up."

"Is she all right?"

"What do you mean, 'Is she all right?'" he said. "You ever seen anybody beat up?"

"How badly is she hurt?" I said.

"She'll recover."

"Who beat her up?"

"Ask her."

We wheeled onto Santa Monica toward West Hollywood. Rafferty drove very economically and very fast. He was strong-looking, deeply tanned, with a strong neck and muscular forearms. He wore a green Lacoste polo shirt, pale Levi's jeans, and blue Tiger running shoes with green crosshatched striping. His face was chiseled and full of character, with a dimple in each cheek and one in the chin. He wore his hair longish and combed back. It was brown and sunlightened. In short he was manly and gorgeous. Except it was all in miniature. He couldn't have been taller than five feet six, and he probably weighed a hundred and fifty.

I said, "It is kind of you not to burden me with information overload. Just looking at me, you could probably tell I need facts in very small doses."

He slammed the car into a left turn where Santa Monica meets Doheny and we were going uphill on Doheny toward Sunset.

Without looking at me, he said, "Don't fuck around with me, Jack, I've handled bigger guys than you."

"And weren't they surprised," I said.

We turned off Doheny just below Sunset and onto Wetherly Drive.

"She wants to see you, so she'll see you," Rafferty said. "But anytime after that, you want to try me out, wise guy, why, start right in."

I didn't seem to have him intimidated.

We stopped in front of a small neat house among many small neat houses on Wetherly Drive. They built close together in L.A. A lot of good-looking vine that I couldn't identify grew over the blank front of the house. We went down the narrow passage between this house and its neighbor. Rafferty unlocked the door and we went in. The floors were polished hardwood, to the right was a large living room. The back wall of the living room was glass and looked out onto a pool and a small cabana that occupied all there was of the backyard. The pool sparkled with blue water—clarified, filtered, and pH-balanced—and the effect in the living room was of space and nature in a remarkably small area. Candy Sloan half sat on the couch in front of the glass wall, her feet up, wearing a blue silk bedjacket with a mandarin collar. One eye was closed; her lip was badly swollen and showed the loose end of a stitch at one corner. There was a darkening lump on her forehead, above the good eye. When I came in, she moved her face slightly. I assumed she was smiling. The movement obviously hurt, and she stopped.

"I guess they were serious," she said. She barely moved her mouth. Her voice was normal and seemed out of place, issuing from the battered face.

"Anything broken," I said.

"No."

"How about the body? Ribs? Anything?"

"They just hit me in the face," she said. "Messed it up."

I nodded. Rafferty had gone to the alcove off the living room and poured coffee from an electric percolator on the sideboard. To his right I could see a stand-up kitchen.

"I should've been here," he said.

"It didn't even happen here, Mickey," she said. "We've been through this. Let's not do it again."

"How about the bozo you hired." Rafferty tossed his chin at me. "Him. Where the hell was he?"

"Mickey!" she said. The force of her saying it made her wince.

He drank some coffee and was quiet, but the cords in his neck were still taut.

I said, "Tell me about it."

She said, "After I dropped you off, I went back to the station. I had to tape a three-minute insert for the six o'clock news. Right after I got through taping, I got a call from someone named Danny. He said he had something hot on the series I'd been doing and wanted to meet me. He wouldn't talk on the phone and said he was being followed. He said he'd meet me in Griffith Park in the zoo parking lot. He said he'd be driving a black van with orange flames painted on it and Nevada plates."

Talking was a bit of an effort for her. She stopped

— 16 —

"And you went, goddamm it, by yourself," Rafferty said. "Why in hell didn't you call me?" He had set his coffee down on the dining table and was grinding his right fist into his left palm as he talked.

"I'm a reporter, Mick," she said. "I am not just a goddamn talking head that reads somebody else's stuff off the crawl."

"You're also my woman," he said.

"No, Mickey. I'm *my* woman."

With his teeth clenched Rafferty said, "Shit," walked into the small kitchen, leaned his hands on the counter, and stared into the sink. The position made his shoulders hunch up.

I walked over to the percolator and poured some coffee into a mug. "Then what?" I said. I sipped some coffee. It was weak.

"I went to Griffith Park. The van was there. I got out of my car and walked over to it. A man got out of the back of the van. I walked over to him and he shoved me into the back, came in after me, and the van started up. While it drove around, the man in the back beat me."

"Did he say anything?"

"Yes. He said, 'I'm not going to kill you this time, I'm going to mess up your face.' And he hit me. And he said, 'If you keep snooping around, I'll kill you.' And then he hit me some more. I covered up as much as I could, but he was much stronger."

"And?"

"And after about ten minutes they dumped me out on the Ventura Freeway and drove off. I never lost consciousness."

"Who found you?"

"Highway patrol. They took me to the hospital and then I got in touch with Mickey, and he came and brought me home."

— 17 —

"Cops get a statement from you?"

"Yes."

"Description of the guy?"

"Yes."

"License number?"

"Yes. But they didn't seem too excited. Said it was probably stolen for the occasion."

I nodded. "Tell me about the guy."

"Short, fat, very strong, balding, black mustache and goatee, tattoos on the knuckles of one hand, and here," she indicated the crotch of her thumb and forefinger, "on the other."

"Know what they said?"

"Jesus Christ." Rafferty had returned from the kitchen. "How is she supposed to remember what they said. The guy's punching her."

I looked at him for a moment. "Mickey," I said, "if you keep annoying me at my work, I'm going to make you wait in the car."

"Try it, you bastard. You won't make me do nothing."

"Mickey," Candy said, stretching out the last vowel. "He has to ask. That's what I hired him for. You're just making it harder."

"Not as hard as I can make it," Mickey said. "You shouldn't have hired him in the first place, big-deal eastern hotshot. He don't know his ass from a freeway out here."

"Mickey," I said.

"You got me," he said to Candy. "You don't need him."

"Mickey," I said a little stronger.

"Sure he's big, but how quick can he move. How far will he go. He don't care about you. He's just a fucking employee."

A tear started down Candy Sloan's cheek. Then another one.

I asked, "Mickey, do I have to prove it?"

He didn't say a word, but he raised his right hand toward me and beckoned me with it slowly, moving his feet slightly as he did so, into a kind of right-angled balance, the left foot pointed at me.

Candy said, "Jesus Christ."

I said, "Listen, Mick. I know what's bothering you. It would bother me. It would bother me even more if I was a subcompact, but there's no point to this."

He gestured at me again, his left arm a rigid diagonal across his body, his knees bent.

"I weigh fifty pounds more than you do. I used to be a fighter. I am good and, more than that, it's what I do. I am a professional. Nobody your size has ever come close."

He slid, almost skittered across the room, and snapped a short chop at the side of my neck where it joins the shoulders. I hunched up the muscle and took the chop. It was good but it was a welterweight chop. He was out of his division.

I pushed out a slow right-hand punch that missed his head by a foot. He pounced on the arm, turned his hip into me, and tried to throw me. I didn't let him. I kept the arm bent so he couldn't work against my elbow and braced my front leg so he couldn't pivot me over his hip. He heaved into his throw and nothing happened. We stood in strained counterpoise for a minute. Then, with my left hand, I took a good hold on his belt at the small of his back and lifted his feet off the ground. At the same time I forced my right arm back in against his neck until I could get a grip on his shirt front. He tried to spin loose, but with his feet off the ground he didn't have a lot of traction. I shifted my feet, arched my back a bit, took a deep breath, and jerked him up over my head, holding him horizontal to the floor. The ceiling in the living room was just high enough.

"Mick," I said, trying to keep my voice easy, as if there was no strain to it, "either we agree to be pals, or I fire you through that window."

I don't think I pulled off the no strain part.

"Quick," I said. My arms felt a little trembly. He wasn't as heavy as a barbell, but he wasn't as nicely balanced either.

"Yes," he said.

I set him down on his feet. He was very flushed, and his breathing was quick and short. He stared at me without any sound but the quick breathing. His eyes were very wide. His nostrils seemed flared and pale. One eyelid trembled.

I waited.

The breathing eased slightly, and he nodded his head, the nods getting smaller and smaller. "Yeah," he said.

I waited.

"Yeah," he said. "Yeah. You can take me." He inhaled big, once. "No way you can't take me." He put out his hand.

I took it. It was hard but small, like him.

Chapter 4

RAFFERTY AND I drank several more cups of the weak coffee, and Candy drank a little fruit juice through a straw in one corner of her mouth, and I tried to find out everything I could about the both of them and movie racketeering.

"I'm a stunt man," Mickey told me.

"And he gets a lot of speaking parts too," Candy said.

Mickey shrugged. "Mostly stunts though, so far," he said.

"You live here?" I said.

He shook his head. "Right now I'm living up in the Marmont, got a nice housekeeping setup there."

"On Sunset?" I said.

"Yeah."

"Place looks like the castle of a low-income Moor?"

Rafferty grinned. "Yeah. That's the place, I guess. I been there a year or so. I'm looking for a place maybe in the Hills somewhere." He looked at Candy. "Or here, a' course. I'd move in here in a minute."

Candy would have smiled softly if she could. As it was, she just looked at the carpet. "Candy's sort of old-fashioned," Rafferty said. "We been going around together for a while, but she still won't move in with me or"—he made a wobbling motion with his hand—"vice versa."

"I go with other men too, Mickey," Candy said.

He looked at the carpet this time.

I said, "Who you got for an eyewitness on this thing?"

Candy nodded her head slightly toward Rafferty.

"You?" I said.

"Yeah," Rafferty said. "Me. I saw the goddamn payoff. I was—"

I put my hand up, palm out. "I'll want to know every detail, but not yet. Are you it?"

"It? Yeah, I'm it. I saw the whole thing."

"I mean, is there any other witness?"

"Sure. Sam Felton, the slug he paid."

"Will either of them talk?"

Candy said no.

"So Mickey is your only talking witness?"

"Yes."

I looked at him. "And you're going to look out for *her*?" I said.

"I'm not scared of them," he said.

"I am," I said. "The limpest pansy in the world can get a gun and put you away without perspiring."

Rafferty shrugged. "I'm not scared," he said again.

"So," I said to Candy. "I am sitting here with everything you've got on the Mob payoffs."

"Well, I have a lot of people to talk with," she said.

"But if a bomb went off in this room right now, the investigation would be over, wouldn't it?"

She and Rafferty looked at each other.

"Wouldn't it?"

"The station would follow up," Candy said.

I breathed deeply. "Okay, let's start at the beginning. Mick, I assume you go first."

"We were shooting a movie on location out in the valley," Rafferty said. "Bike picture called *Savage Cycles*, and I see Felton talking with a guy. I'm behind one of those little commissary trucks, having a Coke and a donut, you know, and they don't really notice me."

"What did the guy look like?" I said.

"Fat guy, bald, had a little beard—you know, a Vandyke—but strong-looking, you know? Hard fat."

I looked at Candy.

"Sound familiar?"

"Maybe," she said.

Rafferty looked back and forth between us. "What did I miss?" he said.

"You were out in the kitchen looking at the sink," I said. "It sounds like the guy that poured it on Candy last night."

"Him?" Rafferty's eyes widened and his mouth thinned. "That fat fuck?" He opened his mouth to say something else, realized he had nothing to say, breathed in instead, and shut his mouth.

"We'll file that information," I said. "Who's Sam Felton?"

"Producer. Studio is Summit."

"And you saw him talking to a fat man?"

"Yeah and the fat guy said, 'Here I am.' And Felton says, 'Here's your money. Same as last week?' And the fat guy says, 'Absolutely.' He says, 'I don't jack up the price. I don't do business that way. You make a deal, you stick with it.' And Felton hands him an envelope, and the fat guy takes it and folds it over and puts it in his hip pocket without looking. And Felton says nothing else. Just stands there. So the fat guy says, 'See you next week. Same time, same station,' and gives him a kind of little salute. You know, like this." Rafferty touched his forehead and flipped his hand away. "Like, 'ta-ta,' you know?"

"Yeah. Did you see what he drove away in?"

"No."

"Why do you think it's a payoff?"

"What else could it be?"

"Did you say anything to Felton?"

"No."

"So for all you know, Felton could be paying off his bookie."

"It wasn't like that," Rafferty said. "I don't know how to explain it, but it was a payoff. There was a threat there. The way the fat guy stood and talked. The way Felton was. There was something going on."

"And you'd heard rumors about payoffs already."

"Yeah, sure. I mean, Candy had mentioned she was looking into it."

"So you were keeping an eye out."

"Sure. But I didn't read anything into it. I'm telling you, this is straight. Besides, look what happened to Candy. Doesn't that prove it?"

"It adds credence," I said.

"I went to see Felton," Candy said. "He denied the entire incident. I talked to other people on the set. They didn't know anything, but I had a sense Felton was covering up something. As if he were scared or guilty."

"Just a feeling, like Rafferty's?"

"Yes. But I'm a reporter; it's a trained feeling. I think they used to call it a hunch in the old Bogart movies."

"And?"

"And I had an appointment scheduled with the head of Summit Studios, Roger Hammond. It was scheduled for today." She paused. "I missed it," she said.

"Did you tell Felton that Rafferty saw him?"

"No. I just said I had an eyewitness."

"Anybody know that Rafferty is it?"

Candy was quiet for a moment. "Just the police and the news director at the station."

"You tell anybody, Mick?"

He shrugged. "Well I asked around a little. People on the crew. Some of the cast, like that."

"So a lot of people know you saw the payoff."

"Well, yeah. So what? I can handle what comes along."

"Be prepared to," I said. "I can look out for her, but you're on your own."

"Don't worry about me," Rafferty said.

"Listen," I said. "I can take you, and there's guys can take me. Don't be such a goddamn rooster all the time. Someone wants to kill you, it's not hard."

"Just 'cause I'd lose doesn't mean I won't fight you," Rafferty said. "I don't have to listen to a lot of cheap shit from you, win or lose."

I nodded. "That's true. I'll give it a rest. But you've got to know what you're dealing with. These aren't tough guys who are trying to prove their manliness, or guys who are interested in who can take who. These are people who will shoot you in the back while you walk up to your door, or guys who will run you over when you're crossing Melrose Avenue on your way to Lucy's El Adobe. They don't care if it hurts. They don't care if it's fair. They care about you being dead and silent. These are people you're supposed to be scared of."

"You be scared of them," Rafferty said. "I got no time for any more goddamn lectures." He looked at Candy Sloan. "I'll be around. You need me, I'll be there." He left the room, walked down the short hall, opened the door, went out, and shut it behind him. Firmly.

Candy and I were quiet. The living room seemed to take on the blue clarity of the pool outside.

Candy said, "He's been small all his life."

"I know," I said.

The walls of the house were thick and stuccoed. No sound came through them. There was only the faint purr of central air conditioning somewhere inside. A single leaf drifted onto the surface of the pool and turned slowly.

"What now?" Candy said.

"Now you rest and I watch you. When you're better, we'll keep that appointment you broke today."

"You and I?"

"You and I."

Chapter 5

CANDY WAS A quick healer. I sat with her for two days while the swelling subsided and the cuts began to heal. I cooked soup for her and whatever I could find in her kitchen for me. The first night I made pasta with fresh vegetables in a thin cream sauce. After that it was downhill. Candy didn't have a rich larder, and by the end of the second day I was reduced to crackers and peanut butter with a side of instant coffee. Nights I slept on the couch; days I read whatever she had handy: Rachel Wallace's new book, *Vogue*, *The Hollywood Reporter*, *Variety*, *Redbook*, a collection of essays by Joan Didion. I wished I'd brought my copy of *Play of Double Senses* with me. It would have impressed the hell out of Candy. I could let drop that it was by the president of Yale, and she'd think I was learned. However, the book was in my suitcase at the Beverly Hillcrest along with my clean shirt and my toothbrush. Candy had a razor, so I was clean-shaven, but my breath was beginning to tarnish my teeth.

Late morning of the third day, I was doing sit-ups with my back on the floor and my feet on the couch when Candy came out of her bedroom dressed, with her hair combed and a good job of makeup that covered a lot of the damage. I was looking at her upside down. She looked very good.

"I'm ready," she said.

"For what?"

"For Roger Hammond, for getting you a real meal,

for going out and getting back to work. Not necessarily in that order."

"No," I said. "Definitely not in that order. First the decent meal."

She smiled, sort of. "Okay," she said. "It's late enough to make it brunch, maybe. Do you always sleep that way?"

"Sit-ups," I said. "Isolates the stomach and saves the back."

"I thought you were supposed to keep your legs straight."

"You were wrong."

She smiled again, sort of, favoring the side where the stitches still pulled. I got up.

"How many do you do?"

"A hundred." I put the gun and holster back on my belt, got my blazer off the back of a chair, and slipped into it. My yellow shirt was in trouble, and my pants were baggy. "How about we go to my hotel while I get a change of clothes and a brush of tooth and then off to some elegant Hollywood bistro for an early lunch."

She nodded. "I'll call a cab. I left my car in Griffith Park."

The cab took us to the Hillcrest, where I showered and shaved and brushed my teeth and put on clean clothes and left the others to be cleaned. I had switched to a light gray blazer, charcoal slacks, white shirt, black and red paisley pocket handkerchief.

"Tie?" I said to Candy Sloan.

She looked as scornful as she could without pulling her stitches.

"I'll try to find a place that requires one before you leave, so you won't have brought one out here in vain."

"I brought several," I said. "Keeps me in touch with my roots. Where shall we eat?"

"I can't eat much. Is there any place you've heard of you'd like to try?"

"Actually I'd like to go back up to the Hamburger Hamlet on Sunset."

"Near my apartment?"

"Yeah."

"After I saw you make that pasta the other night, I thought you were a fancy eater."

"I am. And a plain one. And a big one. I like Hamburger Hamlets."

"All right, but you must let me take you to Scandia when I can eat too."

"I been to Scandia. But I'll go again."

At Hamburger Hamlet I had a frappéed margarita and a large hamburger and a big beer. Candy managed a dish of something called Custard Lulu. Then we took a cab out to Griffith Park and found Candy's car where she had parked it, near the zoo entrance. It was a brown MGB with a chrome luggage rack. She put the top down, and we drove back to Hollywood on the Golden State Freeway then along Los Feliz to Western and then onto Hollywood Boulevard. The sun was bright. The smog was in remission. I was struck, as I always was, with the shabbiness of Hollywood Boulevard. It was a small-town shabbiness: low stucco with paint peeling, burrito stands with plastic Mexicans and plastic cactuses and plastic burros. There were places that sold Hollywood memorabilia and places that sold papaya juice; there were office buildings about the size of those in Pittsfield, Massachusetts, there were gas stations and record stores, and pink-and-yellow motels, and a steady mingle of street kids and tourists.

"Gee," I said, "if things really started booming out here, this could become another Forty-second Street."

"Oh, come on," Candy said. "It's not that bad."

We stopped at a light at Cahuenga Boulevard. A young black man with a haircut like Dorothy Hamill's crossed in front of us. He wore lipstick and mascara. He wore tight pink pants and spike heels, and his fingernails were long and painted silver. With him was a thin blond boy with a tank top and short shorts and translucent shoes with four-inch spikes. He, too, was wearing makeup and jewelry. He carried a small beaded clutch purse. The black kid blew me a kiss. The blond boy yanked at his hand and whispered something, and they hurried across the street.

The light changed, Candy slipped into gear, and we moved on. Behind the thin gray line of buildings and sidewalks the Hollywood Hills rose to the north, green with trees, dotted with color, and beyond them, looking sere, the San Gabriel Mountains. The old Pacific wilderness, barely at bay. We turned left onto Fairfax and headed south past CBS and the Farmers Market, across Wilshire, with the May Company on the corner. Had Mary Livingstone really worked there?

We crossed Olympic and turned right onto Pico. Along Pico there were a lot of kosher markets. Then we slipped up over a hill and down past a Big Boy burger stand and turned into the gate at Summit Studios. Candy showed her press card to the guard at the gate and asked for Roger Hammond. The guard went into his shack to call and came out in a minute and waved us through. To the right of the gate as we drove in was a Victorian street full of false fronts and, beyond that, the superstructure of an old elevated train. Candy turned left past a sound stage and parked in a slot marked VISITORS in front of a two-story building with a balcony across the front.

Summit Studios looked sort of like one of those permanent fairgrounds with a large number of small nondescript buildings scattered about inside a fence. None of the buildings were very new and most of them needed a paint touch up.

We went up the stairs at one end of the balcony and walked halfway down the length of the building to a door with a plaque that said ROGER HAMMOND in simulated-oak Formica. We went in. A rather elderly secretary told us to sit on the couch, Mr. Hammond was on the phone long-distance.

I looked at Candy. "Long-distance," I said soundlessly. She nodded and smiled. "I've never met anyone, when I came to interview them, who was on the phone making a local call," she said softly.

The secretary went back to work. Some phones rang. She answered them. After about ten minutes Roger Hammond appeared at the office door to the left of the secretary and said, "Candy Sloan. I love you on the news."

We stood up.

"Come on inside," Hammond said. "I'm sorry as hell to make you wait. But I was talking long-distance."

I smiled. Candy introduced us. Hammond shook my hand firmly and about half a second longer than he should have. He was a slim, sandy-haired, Irish-looking guy, with a fine lacework of broken veins on his cheeks that looked like a healthy color if you weren't observant. He had a widow's peak with the hair receding substantially on either side of the peak, and the hair was cut short without sideburns. He was dressed Designer Western with boots, dark blue jeans, and a plaid shirt, half unbuttoned. His belt was a wide one of hand-tooled leather with silver mountings. It matched his boots.

"You in TV, Spenser?" he said.

"No."

"Oh?"

"Spenser's helping me on a special assignment, Mr. Hammond. We're looking into the charges of labor racketeering in the film industry."

"I'd heard you were doing a series on that, Candy. Or at least that it was on the boards. Have you got anything yet?"

"I got beaten up several days ago."

"My God, you didn't. Hell, you did, didn't you. I can see the marks, now that you mention it and I'm really looking. God, Candy, that's terrible."

"I'll recover."

"And Spenser," Hammond said. "That's where you come in, isn't it? You are her bodyguard."

I shrugged.

"Sure you are. You've got the build for it. You look like a guy can handle himself. You stay close to this big guy, Candy."

Candy smiled and nodded. "What can you tell me about labor racketeering in the industry, Mr. Hammond?"

"Roger," he said. "Call me Roger."

Candy smiled again and nodded. "What can you tell me?"

Hammond shrugged widely, bringing his hands, palms up, to shoulder level, elbows in. "I wish I could, Candy, but I can't. I don't know a damn thing. I've never encountered any. I've heard rumors, you know, in the industry, but nothing firsthand."

"I've got an eyewitness that said a producer on one of your movies handed an envelope of cash to a thug on the set."

Roger looked at Candy Sloan for a moment. Then he pressed his hands together beneath his chin and touched the underside of his chin with his fingertips. He rocked back in his high-backed executive swivel-chair and gazed at the ceiling. Then he let the chair come forward until his elbows rested on the desk. He dropped his eyes level again at Candy, and with his fingertips still touching his chin, he said, "Candy, that's bullshit."

Then he pointed the still-pressed fingertips at her for emphasis.

Candy shook her head. "No, Roger. It's not bullshit. I have the eyewitness. The producer was Sam Felton. The movie was *Savage Cycles*. Are you telling me you know nothing of this?"

Roger was shaking his head. "Candy, Candy, Candy," he said. "This is bad." He was shaking his head and moving his hands in time with the shake. "This is no good, Candy. This is lousy yellow journalism. Are your ratings that bad?"

"Roger, I've got the eyewitness. Now, I certainly wanted to give you a chance to comment before we go on the air with this."

"Candy, you haven't got anything," Roger said. "You got a new director who's third in the market and he's scared for his job, that's what you got. Nobody in my organization is paying anybody anything. That's my statement. You have an eyewitness, bring him out. Who is it?"

Candy shook her head.

Roger nodded. "Yeah. I thought that's the way it would be, Candy. You have an eyewitness, but he has no name. You and Joe McCarthy." He unpressed his hands and made a repelling gesture, as if to brush away a swarm of gnats.

Candy smiled brightly at him and was silent. He was silent. I was silent. Roger stared at Candy and then glanced at me and then stared at Candy some more. He pressed the hands back together again and rested his chin on them, the fingertips against his mouth. Candy's legs were crossed and her knees were very handsome. So was the line of her thigh beneath the white skirt. Sexism.

"If you have a witness, Candy," Roger said, "I'd like to confront him, or her. If you have real evidence of wrongdoing in my organization, you owe it to me to level with me."

"I think there's danger to the witness," Candy said.

Roger was aghast. He pointed both thumbs at his own chest. "From me? Danger from me? Who the hell do you think I am?"

"So you deny any knowledge of labor racketeering, payoffs, kickbacks, whatever, in Summit Studios," Candy said.

"Absolutely," Roger said. "Categorically. And let me say this, Candy. I resent very much the implication that I might be guilty of complicity. There are libel laws, and I'm going to be talking with our legal people."

"Sam Felton had to get the money from somewhere," Candy said. "I assume he wasn't paying out of pocket. Could you put me in touch with your financial officer, Roger? Treasurer, comptroller, whatever you call him here."

"For God's sake, I will not. Candy, this has gone far enough. I've tried to cooperate, but you are not willing to be reasonable. You come in here and make wild charges and ask for the name of our treasurer." He looked at me, leaning forward a little. "Spender, what the hell am I going to do with her?"

"It's not just that you got my name screwed up," I said, "it's how you enlisted me in your cause. What are we sensible guys going to do with this silly broad. That's where you lost me."

"Geez, I'm bad with names," Hammond said. "I must have misunderstood, what is your name again?"

"Spenser," I said. "Like in Edmund."

"I'm sorry, Spenser. Of course. I don't mean to get sexist here. I'm just asking you for an opinion. You look like a guy's been around, Spense. Can't you talk some sense to her?"

"Not my job," I said. "If I were you though, I'd take her seriously."

"I'll take her seriously," Hammond said. "I'll take you both seriously when you give me some evidence besides a goddamn ghost witness. Do you have any?"

"I have enough to make me look for more," Candy said.

"To go fishing, you mean. If you had anything, you wouldn't be here."

"But there is some," Candy said. "I just haven't dug it up yet, is that what you're saying?"

"Don't put words in my mouth, you bitch," Hammond said.

"Roger," I said. "I signed the standard bodyguard's contract, you know, to protect her against sticks and stones and broken bones. I'm not sure names are covered. My inclination, however, is to interpret the contract loosely."

"Spense, are you threatening me?"

"I guess so, Rog. I guess I'm saying you shouldn't call her names, or I will tie a knot in your Ralph Lauren jeans."

Hammond half rose with his hands flat on the desktop. He leaned forward, carrying his weight on his stiff arms, and said, "That's it. This interview is at an end. And I fully intend to let the station manager and KNBS know just what kind of totally unprofessional job was done here today."

"His name is Wendall B. Tracey," Candy said.

"I know his name," Hammond said.

We were all on our feet now. Candy opened the door. We went out.

Chapter 6

As we walked back toward the car, Candy said, "Want a drink at the commissary?"

"Is there a chance I'll see Vera Hruba Ralston?"

"No."

"Well, I'll go anyway. Maybe we'll see a clue there."

We walked across an open area, past a sound stage and two buildings that looked like barracks, and there was the commissary. It was a pale low stucco building with a small flagstone veranda across the front, facing inward onto a small lawn among the buildings. Inside was a high ceiling, and around the walls, in living Technicolor, were painted a bunch of mythological-looking women with harps and such.

"The nine Muses?" I said to Candy.

"Could be," Candy said. "I didn't know there were nine."

"Same as a baseball team," I said.

"I could use a drink," Candy said. "What would be good. How about a margarita?"

"Salt may hurt."

"You're right. I'll have a martini."

I had a beer.

"What do you think?" Candy said after she'd sipped at the martini. At the table next to us people I vaguely recognized were having drinks and sandwiches and laughing often. The cast of a television show, but I couldn't remember which.

"I think Roger's lying."

"Why?"

"Well," I drank some beer and watched a starlet in a very tight dress sit down at a table to my right. She showed a lot of thigh as she slid into the chair. I'd seen her in a movie somewhere. A Western.

"Well what?" Candy said.

"Oh, I was admiring the presence of that actress."

"You were admiring the inside of her right thigh."

"See what Hollywood's come to," I said. "That's what we call presence now."

Candy put the olive from her martini in her mouth and very carefully chewed it. She winced slightly.

"It's the brine it's cured in," I said. "It'll nip you till you heal completely. Rinse it with a little martini."

"Why do you think Roger Hammond is lying?" Candy said.

"You talked to Felton, right?"

She nodded, running the martini around in her mouth.

"There's no way he wouldn't have told Hammond that you accused him. If he were innocent, he'd tell Hammond, because he'd want his backing in cutting down the bad P.R. If he were guilty, he'd want to get his story told before you got to Hammond. He'd know either way that Hammond would be next on your list. Yet Hammond acted like he'd never heard the accusation. That's not reasonable."

"Maybe Felton thought by having me beaten up, I wouldn't go to Hammond, and the story would die right there."

"Possibly, but he's still got to sweat the unidentified eyewitness. Scaring you off may not scare him off."

A plump blond woman in a purple dress and gold high-heeled shoes stopped at the table and leaned over Candy.

"Candy, how are you? A hot news story?" She smiled and looked at me. "Or maybe a hot date?"

"Agnes, good to see you. Sit down," Candy said. "Let me buy you a drink. Spenser, this is Agnes Rittenhouse."

"How do you do," Agnes said. "Aren't you a manly looking chap?"

"It's because my heart is pure," I said.

"Oh," Agnes said, "how disappointing." She sat down and ordered a piña colada. Candy and I had another round.

"Agnes does publicity for the studio," Candy said to me.

"The pay isn't much," Agnes said, "but I get to keep all the men I can catch."

She was plump without being exactly fat. Just shapely on a larger scale. She had a Cupid's-bow mouth and thin arching eyebrows that she must have plucked often. Her hair was brass-colored and she wore a lot of makeup.

The waiter brought the drinks. "Anything I can help you with?" Agnes said. She drank half her piña colada in a swallow.

"Maybe. Mr. Spenser is visiting me from the East and was interested in how a studio works. I wondered if there's anyone we can talk to in the finance office. Who's your chief finance officer?"

"Are you a reporter too, Mr. Spenser? You're too macho to be an accountant."

"Yes, I am," I said. "I work for a sister station in Boston—same owner, Multi Media—and I'm out doing some soft stuff for the early news. You know, visits with the stars, a look inside the glamor capital of the world, how the movie business runs."

Agnes finished her piña colada and looked automatically for the waiter. "Well, big boy," she said. "If you get tired of that and want to be a gigolo, I can promise you steady work."

"I'd probably have to get my nose straightened,"

I said, "and brush up on my fox-trot. But while I'm doing that, could we get an appointment with your finance officer?"

Agnes started to say something and stopped and looked over my shoulder. I turned, and Roger Hammond was there with three security guards in uniform.

"You are not welcome here," Hammond said to Candy.

Agnes opened her eyes very wide. "Roger," she said, "the media—"

"She is not welcome," Hammond said harder, looking at Agnes.

"What are you afraid we'll find out?" Candy said.

"This is my studio. You are an unhealthy intrusion. Either you leave, or I'll have you removed."

The security guard closest to Hammond was wearing sergeant stripes on his uniform. He was a fortyish black man with graying hair and a lot of scar tissue around his eyes. He was looking at me. I looked back. He had big hands, the knuckles enlarged some, and thick wrists. As he looked at me he licked his lips thoughtfully, the tip of his tongue just showing under a thick gray-speckled mustache.

I looked at the other two guards. They were white, kids no more than twenty-two, and scrawny-looking. One had port-wine birthstains on his right cheek and neck. I could ignore them.

The black man would be trouble.

We looked at each other and he smiled slowly. Candy was saying to Hammond something about freedom of the press. Hammond was saying, "I want you out, I want you out." Agnes had moved back slightly from the table and was watching it all, trying to edge around so she'd be standing with Hammond. She kept looking at me and at the black guard and back at me. Her eyes were shiny.

Most of the people in the commissary were turning

now and looking over. Hammond turned to the black man and said, "Ray, escort them out."

Ray asked, "Him too?"

"Of course."

"He ain't no TV guy," Ray said.

"I know that," Hammond said.

"If he don't want to go, I'm going to have to break things," Ray said.

"For heaven's sake, Ray. There's three of you," Hammond said.

Ray looked briefly at the other two guards. He looked at me. "They can take the woman," he said. He stood easily, his hands relaxed, palms cupped slightly, one foot slightly forward of the other. I was still sitting. I said to Candy, "Are we going to resist?"

She shook her head. "No," she said. "I'm in the business of discovering news and reporting it. I do not wish to make it."

Agnes said to me, "You're not in TV?"

The black guard chuckled softly. Hammond said, "He's a hired bodyguard, Agnes. A strong-arm man."

"Strong arm," I said to the black man.

"I don't doubt it," he said. "We all going?"

"Roger, we'd better talk about this," Agnes said. "Can I stop by your office?"

"No," Hammond said. He pointed a finger at Candy Sloan and then pointed the same finger at the commissary door. Dramatic. You could tell he was creative. Candy nodded at me. I got up slowly and as I did Ray moved just out of jab range with a small economical shuffle that made the movement barely noticeable. A waiter hovered uncertainly around us with a bill. Hammond took it and put it in his pocket, and the waiter ducked back and disappeared. We began to walk toward the door, Candy in front, then me, Ray beside me, the two guards behind him.

"See that they leave the grounds," Hammond said. "And see that they don't come back."

"We'll have to go dwell in the plains," I said to Candy. "East of Eden."

"Sure," she said. She didn't look amused.

We left the commissary. "You parked where?" Ray said.

Candy told him.

"You ever fight on the Coast?" Ray said to me.

"Not this one," I said.

He nodded. "Figured you wasn't local," he said. "I never got East."

When we got to Candy's MG, I held the door for her while she slid in. Ray and his assistant leaned against the side of a blue and gold studio security car parked up on the grass behind us. I went around and got in beside Candy. She started up, shifted, and off we went. The security car followed us to the gate, and then we were back out on Pico, heading east. Candy was silent.

"Too bad," I said. "I think Agnes was smitten with me."

"If you wear pants, Agnes is smitten with you," Candy said.

"Oh."

Candy glanced over and smiled. "Well, maybe she was more smitten with you than with others."

"I thought so," I said.

Chapter 7

CANDY TURNED LEFT onto La Cienega.

"Where now?" I said.

"We're going to see an agent I used to sleep with. He knows more about Hollywood, capital *H*, than anyone in town."

"Mind if I ask him how it was?" I said.

"How what was?"

"When he used to sleep with you."

"You find it shocking that I mention it casually?"

"No, but it seems a little contrived."

"You mean a little too casually sophisticated?"

"Yeah."

She was silent. I thought, peeking at her sideways, that she might have been blushing slightly. We crossed Olympic. Behind us a blue 1970 Pontiac with a black vinyl roof came out of Olympic and turned up La Cienega. It passed a car and swung in behind us. It was still behind us at Wilshire. And it was still behind us at San Vincente.

"Take San Vincente," I said to Candy. "And go back onto La Cienega at Beverly Boulevard."

"No left turn," she said.

"Take it anyway," I said.

She turned onto San Vincente. "You doing some sight-seeing?"

"Maybe. There's a car behind us. I want to see if he's following."

Candy checked the rearview mirror. "Old blue Pontiac?"

"Yes."

We crossed the intersection at Third with the Pontiac still behind us. He had dropped back a little. There were two cars between us. San Vincente Boulevard slants northwest for a short way across the more conventional Los Angeles grid from Pico Boulevard to Melrose Avenue. It crosses La Cienega between Wilshire Avenue and Third Street. At Beverly we turned right and went three blocks east, then left, and we were back heading north on La Cienega. When we crossed Melrose, I checked behind us and the blue Pontiac was there.

Candy looked at me.

"Okay," I said, "so someone is following us. It would be good to know who."

"What do you suppose he thought we were doing with that little maneuver on San Vincente?"

"Unless he's an idiot, he thought we had spotted him and were trying to make sure he was really following us."

"So now he knows we know."

"Yeah."

"He doesn't seem to care."

"That's right."

"What's that mean?"

"It might mean he's going to make a move on us. It might mean he is so interested in what we're doing that he doesn't care about stealth. It might mean he's a cop."

"A cop?"

"Cops don't give a damn about anything sometimes," I said.

"What shall we do?"

"We need a place . . . go east on Melrose then down Fairfax to the Farmers Market."

The Pontiac stayed with us now, openly, no dodging behind cars; it was right behind us. I turned in my seat and rested my chin on my forearms and studied over the open rear deck of the MG.

"There are two of them. Apparently they've dumped the Firebird and the van," I said to Candy. "The one in the passenger seat is balding. He has a black mustache and goatee. It's hard to tell while he's sitting in the car, but he appears to be fat and strong. Does that sound familiar?"

"Oh, my God," Candy said. She cleared her throat.

"It's okay," I said. "This time we've got them outnumbered."

"There's two of them."

I looked at her and flexed my bicep in a physical-culture pose.

"Oh," she said, "I see what you're saying. I'm sorry, but I'm scared. This time what if they mean to kill me?"

"That's what the Sound of the Golden West is paying me for," I said. "When we get to the Farmers Market, pull in close to one of the doors and park, illegally if you need to. Just don't waste any time. Then jump out and run inside, and go in the nearest ladies' room. You know your way around in there?"

"Oh, sure."

"Okay. The ladies' room nearest the entrance we go in. Stay there till I yell for you. I'll open the door and yell."

"You may be arrested as a Peeping Tom." She sounded strained but she was trying.

"You'll swear my eyes were shut tight all the time," I said.

She smiled, though not very wide, and said, "Okay. While I'm hiding in the ladies' room, what are you going to do?"

— 44 —

"I'm going to consult with our groupies here. See if I can get a little information."

The Pontiac was drawing closer.

"Move this thing faster," I said to Candy. "I need a little space between us when we get to the Market."

The MG speeded up as we went down Fairfax. The Pontiac hung in behind us. "You can't outrun it," I said to Candy, "but this thing can outmaneuver it. Slip in and out of traffic a little."

"Spenser, I bought this because it was cute, not because it was hot. I don't know how to stunt-drive."

"Well, do what you can. I don't want them to make a run at us right here on Fairfax."

She bit her lip and tromped down on the accelerator and jockied the little sports car in between a truck and a Lincoln that looked like a truck. The Pontiac edged out around the truck and then fell back in behind it. Candy passed the Lincoln on the inside and got honked at by a red-faced man wearing a pink shirt and smoking a cigar. We screeched into the parking lot on the north side of the Farmers Market, cutting across the traffic recklessly and causing several more horns to blow.

The store section of the Farmers Market was a rambling white low building surrounded by parking lots just south of CBS Studios on the corner of Fairfax Avenue and Third Street. There were cars parked all around the building, and Candy jammed the MG into the walkway leading to one of the entrances, and we jumped out and headed into the market. Just inside the door there was a stand selling barbecue and down the aisle from that was a sign that said REST ROOMS. I pointed at it, and Candy went for it at as brisk a walk as one could muster. I went with her till I saw her go in and then I faded behind a stand that sold Mexican food and moved down the aisles of food stalls

— 45 —

and produce stands, watching the entrance where we'd come in. I saw the fat man. Candy was right. He was fat, but you weren't fooled. He was strong too.

He looked around. I moved down the aisle away from him, past a stand that sold blackberry pie, my mouth watering briefly, then I went past a Chinese-food concession and into the parking lot in front, around the corner from where we'd entered.

The Pontiac was double-parked between the market and the souvenir shop that sold Mexican jewelry and leather cowboy hats and pictures of the Griffith Park Observatory sealed inside a transparent plastic square. Candy's MG was sitting there in the walkway near it. People skirted it to get into the market, shaking their heads; a man suggested to his wife that the driver was an asshole. I felt he'd made his judgment on insufficient evidence.

The driver of the Pontiac was standing leaning against the car with his arms folded on the roof. He was tall and blond with longish hair combed back in a stiff sweep. He had a dark tan and a thick mustache that turned up slightly at the ends. He wore a white shirt with epaulets and a pocket on the left sleeve. It was half unbuttoned. He had two slim gold chains around his neck. The bottom half was bleached white straight-leg cords worn over hand-tooled cowboy boots. His waist was narrow, but his upper body had the thickened look of a weight lifter.

I walked up behind him, stepping softly.

"Are you Troy Donahue?" I said.

He turned his head slowly and looked at me. His skin glowed with a healthy tan. He smelled of Brut and hairspray. There was wax on his mustache.

"Fuck off," he said.

I hit him a firm left hook that tilted his chin back and followed with a right cross that knocked him flat on his back. When he got his eyes focused, I had the barrel of my gun just touching the tip of his nose.

I said, "This is a public place, Troy. Soon somebody will call the cops, and they'll come and it will be awkward. So you tell me real quick why you were following me or I'll blow a hole in the middle of your face."

"I ain't Troy Donahue," he said.

"You're not Albert Einstein either, I guess. But quick"—I shoved the gun against his nose, bending the tip of it in on his upper lip—"why were you following me?" I thumbed the hammer back. There was no need to. It was a double-action piece, but the gesture always looked good.

"I'm day labor, man," Troy said. "I just got hired to drive and help out if there was a hassle."

"Who hired you?"

"Him." Troy pointed with his eyes. "Franco, the fat guy."

"Franco what?"

"I don't know, you know how a guy is. You see him around, you just know his name."

"Franco his first or last name?"

"I don't know."

A ways off I heard a siren. I put the gun back under my coat, got in the Pontiac, started up, and drove away. In the rearview mirror I saw Troy get up and head toward the market. On the seat next to me was a Colt .32 automatic, half-hidden under a newspaper.

I rammed the Pontiac between a wine-tasting shop and the rear of the Market, out across Third Street, through the lot of a shopping center and out onto a side street that led down toward Wilshire. About a block past the shopping center was a kind of a housing development that spread out around a central circle. I parked there, put on my sunglasses, took off my jacket, pulled my shirttails out to cover my hip holster, and stuffed the Colt in my belt in front under the shirt. I went down a little side street and came out on Fairfax. I folded my coat and put it down on the grass along the sidewalk, then I walked back up toward the Farmers Market. My experience with eyewitnesses told me that I had concealed my identity all I needed to. They'd seen a neat man in a gray jacket with no shades. I was now a sloppy man with his shirt out and no jacket wearing sunglasses. I came in the Market from the Third Street side. It wasn't very busy. I didn't see the fat man. The police siren would have made him fade. His buddy Troy had probably cut through the Market and screwed into the neighborhood south of Third. There was some activity around the doors on the far side of the market. That's where the cops would be: *What happened? There were these guys fighting, one had a gun. Where are they now? I don't know. One drove away. What did they look like? Short. Tall. Fat. Thin. Blond. Black. Old. Young. Who called? I don't know. Swell.*

I got to the door of the ladies' room, pushed it partway open, and yelled, "Hey, Candeee."

She came out before I stopped yelling.

"For God's sake what's going on?" she said.

"I'll tell you later. Go get your car. If a cop speaks to you, smile at him. Show him your press credentials. Ask what's going on. Wiggle your ass at him if you feel that's appropriate. Then, when you can, drive down Fairfax, toward Wilshire. I'll be walking along. Stop and I'll get in, and I'll explain while we go see that agent you used to sleep with."

She gave me a hard look but did what I told her.

Chapter 8

I GOT MY jacket back. It was right where I left it and I had it slung debonairly over one shoulder when Candy Sloan pulled up to the curb and honked her horn once. I got in.

"Any trouble?" I said.

"No. One of the police recognized me and just said I shouldn't park there. I smiled and wiggled and off I went."

"Good,"' I said. "Let's go see your priapic agent."

"Why don't you let up on that," Candy said. "I regret the remark."

I nodded. Candy turned east on Wilshire and we went past the L.A. County Museum of Art and the La Brea Tar Pits. At La Brea Avenue Candy turned north.

"What was all the excitement about? What happened to the men who were following us?" Candy said.

I told her about Troy Donahue and the fat man. I also got my shirt tucked in and the Colt stored in the glove compartment of the MG.

"Know how to use one of those?" I said.

"No."

"I'll show you. It might be useful knowledge."

She took in a deep sigh and let it out. "I suppose so. Whose gun is that?"

"I took it away from Troy."

"Isn't it awfully small?"

"Yes."

Straight up La Brea the Hollywood Hills rose like

a clumsy flat in an amateur play. We turned left on Sunset, and drove west toward Beverly Hills. Below us Los Angeles stretched out flat and far. The modern skyscrapers downtown around Figueroa and Sixth streets caught the lowering slant of the afternoon sun and glistened above the herd of low California buildings that filled the L.A. basin. I'd never seen an urban place where the contours of the natural land were still so visible, where the memory of how it was remained so insistent.

Sunset got quite flossy down toward the West Hollywood–Beverly Hills line: small stucco buildings with glass and brass and limned oak decor, restaurants with fake antique doors, boutiques, two-story bungalows with the names of production companies and agents in gold leaf on the doors, an occasional high rise.

Past Robertson, near the top of Doheny, Candy pulled into an open meter. It was only a short walk to Hamburger Hamlet. We'd lunched early. I could claim it was time for high tea. I looked at Candy. She seemed sort of grim. I figured my high tea suggestion wouldn't seem businesslike to her. I suppressed it.

"In downtown Boston," I said, "you can never find a parking meter open."

"That's true in downtown Los Angeles too," she said. "But I'll bet you could in the Boston equivalent of Beverly Hills."

"The Boston equivalent of Beverly Hills is a shopping mall in Chestnut Hill," I said. "They have a parking lot."

We walked to a two-story white building with a small canopied entrance that looked like a funeral parlor. Across the top of the canopy it said: THE MELVIN ZEECOND AND TRUMAN FINNERTY AGENCY.

"Here," Candy said. We went in. There was a receptionist on a switchboard just inside the door in a small hallway, behind a glass partition.

"I'm Candy Sloan," Candy said to the receptionist. "Is Zeke in?"

The receptionist asked us to take a seat in the foyer. We did. The foyer was oval shaped. Big enough for two upholstered gray couches and four or five leather-covered wooden-armed chairs. There were copies of *Daily Variety* and *People* magazine on a coffee table in front of one of the couches. The ceiling was slightly domed and some fluorescent bulbs along the bottom of the dome behind some molding lighted the place indirectly. The place had been recently painted, and in spots along the molding the painters hadn't scraped the previous paint adequately.

Several corridors ran off of the foyer, and I could see offices opening off of them. Everyone I could see seemed to be talking on the phone. A secretary in a green dress with the skirt slit to the thigh came out of one of the corridors and said, "Miss Sloan?"

Candy said, "Yes."

"Zeke's on the phone long-distance," the secretary said. "He'll be with you as soon as he can."

I grinned at the dome. "How quickly they forget," I murmured.

Candy said, "Just shut up."

The secretary said, "I beg your pardon."

Candy said, "I was talking to him. We'll wait."

The secretary and her slit skirt swished off down the corridor.

"Long-distance," I said.

"Shut up."

"Probably if it were a local call, he'd hang right up and be out here."

"Shut up."

"Probably be swirling a little white Bordeaux in a silver wine bucket."

"Champagne," Candy said.

We were quiet. No one else was in the waiting room.

I had the feeling everyone else called up. The waiting room was probably for deliveries.

A tall woman with prominent teeth and a three-piece gray suit hurried through the foyer and leaned her head into the open door of the office nearest us down the right-hand hallway. With the suit she was wearing a poppy shirt with a small pin-collar and a narrow black knit tie. She hurried back across the foyer. Then a man appeared in the middle corridor and said, "Candy, honey, this is terrific."

He was tall and slim and had snow-white hair and a youthful face with a black mustache. He was darkly tanned and wore a glen plaid suit and vest with a black shirt open at the throat. He might have been forty or he might have been sixty. A small tangle of white hair showed at the V of his shirt. On the little finger of his left hand he wore a gold ring with a red stone.

"Hello, Zeke."

"Come on in."

She followed him down the corridor; I followed her. When we got to his office, she introduced me. We shook hands. He had a strong grip, but I was holding back.

He smiled at me. "A little old, I think, to be with the Rams," he said. "Stunt man?"

"Sort of," I said.

Candy said, "Spenser is helping me on an investigative series we're doing."

The office was on the first floor and had a little bay window framed with gray drapes that looked out onto Sunset and people on the sidewalk. There were several autographed pictures of actors on the wall and a bookcase-liquor cabinet-stereo set up along one side of the room. Besides a desk with two phones there were two more of the leather-and-wood sitting room chairs. Zeke was behind his desk, we sat in the chairs. The walls were pale gray, the rug was charcoal.

"Candy." Zeke folded his hands on the desk and leaned forward slightly. "How can I help?"

"I need to know some things about Summit Pictures and Roger Hammond."

Zeke kept his hands folded and leaned back in the chair. The movement slid his hands to the edge of the desk.

He said, "Oh?"

"I need it, Zeke. This is important to me."

"Tell me about it."

She did, everything, except the name of her eye-witness. Zeke sat motionless and looked right at her as she talked.

"And if you break this thing open, it will mean a lot to your career," he said when she was through.

"Absolutely," Candy said. "More air time, more feature stuff, more hard-news assignments, maybe a shot at the networks, who knows. I know that it's still hard for a woman to push her way up through the men in the news business. And if I can't handle a real story when it starts to break, it will be much harder."

Zeke nodded. He looked at me. I had my arms crossed and was watching the occasional pedestrian go by on Sunset. "That explains the big fella here," Zeke said.

"He's a bodyguard," Candy said. "He's not doing the investigating for me."

"No skill-work," I said, "just heavy lifting."

Zeke nodded. He tucked his lower lip under the edge of his mustache and sucked down on his upper lip.

"An agent doesn't make it out here by gossiping to the press about studio heads," he said.

"I know. It's background. I'll never quote you," Candy said.

Zeke sucked on his upper lip some more.

"It's not just the career, Zeke," Candy said. "It's . . .

the fat son of a bitch beat me up. Dragged me into a van and punched and slapped me and threw me out on the Ventura Freeway like an empty Coke can."

The tall woman with the gray suit stuck her head in the door.

She said, "Excuse me, Zeke, but we're going to screen those clips that Universal sent over." She talked with her teeth clenched and without moving her lips. She was like someone Central Casting had sent over to play an Ivy League executrix. I looked at Candy. She wasn't looking at me. She was looking hard at Zeke. Zeke looked at his chronograph. He looked at Candy.

"Go ahead without me, Mary Jane, I can't leave right now."

One point for old Zeke.

"Want us to reschedule?" the executrix said.

Zeke shook his head and made a slight dismissal gesture with the first three fingers of his right hand.

"I'll give you a file memo of my reaction, Zeke," she said, and pulled her head out of the room. Zeke unclasped his hands and rubbed the bridge of his nose with his thumb and forefinger.

"I'm ass-deep in file memos from Mary Jane," he said.

"She got lockjaw?" I asked.

"No," Zeke said. "She went to Smith."

"What about Summit Studios, Zeke?" Candy said.

He nodded at the door. "Could you close that for me," he said. I got up and closed it.

"And Roger Hammond," Zeke said when the door was closed.

Candy nodded.

"I have heard," Zeke said, "that Hammond got into a lot of fiscal difficulty about five years ago and that somebody in a West Coast Mob family bailed him out."

"Who was the mobster?"

"I don't know."

"Personal or business?" Candy said.

"Business. I heard he mismanaged the studio into an economic pit. He had a lot of money out that did not return investment. He bought a lot of bad properties, packaged them wrong, and they bombed. He couldn't get the product into the theaters after a while. So then I heard he started embezzling from the profitable releases to cover the losses on the bombs, and he started juggling books so that his bosses wouldn't know how bad it was."

"His bosses are who?" Candy said.

"Oceania Limited: Petroleum, Timber, Mineral Processing, and Moviemaking." Zeke shook his head and made the kind of mouth movement you make when you've gotten ashes on your tongue.

"Oceania catch on?" I said. Candy looked at me and frowned. "Oops," I said. "Am I in your space?"

Candy shook her head in small annoyance and looked at Zeke.

"Did they?" she said.

"Catch on?" he shrugged. "Hammond is still there."

"Because he got money from a mobster to cover the losses?"

Zeke nodded. "That's what I hear."

"What did the mobster get?" Candy said.

"I don't know," Zeke said. "It's not the kind of thing I want to know too much about. What I hear about mobsters they must have got something."

"They got Hammond," I said.

"What do you mean 'got'?" Candy said.

"Like Mephistopheles 'got' Faust," I said. "But they won't wait to collect."

"Why are you so sure?" Candy said.

"It's too easy. They bail him out and now they own him, and they're in the movie business and he fronts it. Dirty money goes in, clean money comes out."

"You think the Mob controls Summit Pictures?" Candy said.

"If what Zeke hears is right, I can almost promise you," I said.

Candy looked at Zeke. "What do you think?" she said.

He shrugged. "He'd know more about that than I would, I think."

Candy looked back at me. "It makes sense, doesn't it."

I nodded.

Zeke said, "I will deny ever saying anything about this, Candy."

"You won't have to," Candy said. "I'll never mention you. You can trust me."

He nodded. "There's no one else I would have talked to," he said.

"It would be nice to believe that, Zeke," she said.

They looked silently at each other for a while and I looked out the window. Then Candy said, "Thank you, Zeke," and we got up and left.

Chapter 9

"I WANT TO go to dinner," Candy said, "and I want you to escort me."

"I'll risk that," I said.

We went to The Palm on Santa Monica. The walls were covered with clumsy murals of show-biz celebrities in caricature. But my plate was covered with medium-rare butterflied lamb chops and asparagus with hollandaise.

I drank a little beer. "You have a plan?" I said.

"Keep talking and asking," she said. She ate a scallop carefully. "That's what investigative reporting is. Talking, asking; asking, talking."

I nodded. "Who you going to ask and talk with next?"

"Somebody at Oceania."

"Got a name?"

"No. Any suggestions?"

"Why not the president. Might as well get as close as we can to God." I ate some lamb chop.

"I agree. We'll do it tomorrow morning," she said.

A man next to us—dark suit, white French cuffs, large oynx cuff links—said to the waiter, "Tell Frank I'm out here and tell him to give me that center cut he's been saving."

The waiter, an old man with no expression on his face, said, "Yes, sir. How you want that?"

The middle-aged man said, "How do I want it? Frank knows damn well how I want it. Barely dead."

He raised both hands as if measuring a fish while he spoke.

The waiter said, "Rare. Very good, sir." He went away.

The middle-aged man was with a smooth red-haired young woman in a low-necked green dress and a younger man in a gray three-piece suit and a striped tie. They were all drinking red wine.

"Wait'll you see the piece of beef Frank'll have for me," the middle-aged man said. He looked around to see if I was impressed. He had a diamond pinkie ring on his right hand. "You shoulda had a piece, honey," he said to the woman beside him. She smiled and said yes, she probably should, but she could never eat all that. The guy in the gray suit drank his wine rapidly.

I said to Candy, "Would it violate the terms of my contract if I told that guy to shut up about his goddamn roast beef?"

Candy smiled. "I think you're just supposed to concentrate on protecting me. I think you're supposed to give etiquette instructions on your own time."

When we left, the middle-aged man was eating a piece of rare rib roast and talking with his mouth full about the weaknesses of French cooking, and the problems he'd had with it on his last trip to Europe.

With a little pull from the Sound of the Golden West we had gotten Candy, under a phony name, the room adjoining mine at the Hillcrest. As we drove, the streets in Beverly Hills were as still as an empty theater in the night. The lobby was deserted.

We were alone in the elevator.

At her door I took her key and opened the door first. The room was soundless. I reached in and turned on the light. No one was there. I opened the bathroom and looked behind the shower glass. I opened the sliding closet door. I looked under the bed. No one was there either.

Candy stood in the doorway watching me. "You're serious, aren't you."

"Sure. Just because it's corny to hide under the bed doesn't mean someone wouldn't do it."

I slid open the doors to the small balcony. No one there either. I went to the door connecting my room with hers. It was locked. "Before you go to bed, remember to unlock this," I said. "No point me being next door if I can't get to you."

"I know," she said. "I'll unlock it now."

"No," I said. "Wait until I've checked out the room."

"Oh," she said. "Of course."

"I'll go over now. Lock the corridor door behind me and chain it. I'll yell through the connecting door if it's okay."

She nodded. I went out, went into my room, and made sure it was empty. The connecting door was bolted from each side. I slid my bolt back and said, "Okay, Candy."

I heard her bolt slip and the door opened. She was on the phone, the phone cord stretched taut across the bed as she had to reach to unbolt the door. As she opened the door she said, "Thank you," into the phone and hung up.

"I just ordered a bottle of cognac and some ice," she said. "You want a drink?"

"Sure," I said. "Your place or mine?"

"This isn't a pass," she said. "I'd just like to sit on the balcony and sip some brandy and talk quietly. I'm a little scared."

I thought about the balcony. We were seven floors up, on a corner; there was no balcony beyond us. The one next to us on the other side was mine. The ones on the next floor were directly above. It would be a hard shot. And you'd have to have been smart enough or lucky enough to get a room above us with the right angle. I said, "Okay, the balcony is good. But we'll turn the lights off. No point in making a better target than we need to."

The bellhop brought the bottle of Rémy Martin, a soda siphon, two glasses, and a bucket of ice. I watched while Candy added in a tip and signed the bill. Then we shut off the lights and took the tray out onto the balcony.

Lights speckled the Hollywood Hills. There was a faint sound of music from the rooftop lounge above us. On Beverwil Drive a cab idled. I opened the bottle and poured two drinks over ice with a small squirt of soda. Candy took one and sipped it. She had kicked her shoes off and now she put her stockinged feet up on the low cement railing of the balcony. She was wearing a plum-colored wraparound dress, and the skirt fell away halfway up her thigh. I stood leaning against the doorjamb and watched the other balconies. Mostly.

"Tell me about yourself, Spenser."

"I was born in a trunk," I said, "in the Princess Theatre in Pocatello, Idaho."

"I know it's a corny question, but it's still a real one. What are you like? How did you end up in such a strange business?"

"I got too old to be a Boy Scout," I said.

I could smell flowers in the soft California evening. Candy sipped her brandy. The ice clinked gently in the glass as she rolled it absently between her hands. Mingled with the smell of flowers was the smell of Candy's perfume.

"That's not an entirely frivolous answer, is it?" she said.

"No."

"You want to help people."

"Yes."

"Why?"

"Makes me feel good," I said.

"But why this way? Guns, fists, hoodlums?"

"Because they're there," I said.

"You're laughing at me, but I will proceed. It's why I'm a good reporter. I keep asking. Why not be a doctor or a schoolteacher or"—she spread her hands, the glass in one of them—"you get the idea."

"Systems," I said. "The system gets in the way. You end up serving the medical profession or public education. I tried the cops for a while."

"And?"

"They felt I was too creative."

"Fired?"

"Yes."

Candy poured herself another drink. I squirted in some soda. "Are you attracted to violence?" she asked.

"Maybe. To a point. But it's also that I'm good at it. And there's a need for someone who's good at it. Someone needs to keep that fat guy from smacking you around."

"But what if you meet someone who's better?"

"Unthinkable," I said.

"No," she said. "It isn't unthinkable at all. You're too thoughtful a man not to have thought of it."

"How about *unlikely* then?"

"Maybe, but what happens? How do you feel?"

I took in a deep breath. "Talking about myself seriously has always seemed a little undignified," I said. "But . . ." The cab on Beverwil got a fare. Must be going a long way. I had the feeling Beverly Hills closed at sundown.

"But what?" Candy said.

"But the possibility that you'll meet somebody better is part of"—I gestured with my right hand—"if that possibility didn't exist," I said, "it would be like playing tennis with the net down."

Candy drank her brandy and soda and got another from the tray, and when she had the drink rebuilt, she looked at it and then looked at me. She took a sip and then held the glass against her chin with both hands and looked at me some more.

"It's a kind of game," she said.

"Yes."

"A serious game," she said.

I was quiet. I poured a small splash of brandy in my glass and added a lot of ice and a lot of soda. Be embarrassing to pass out in front of the client.

"But why can't you play that same game inside a system? In a big organization?"

"You're talking about yourself now," I said.

"Perhaps," she said. The final *s* slushed just barely.

On the rooftop someone had apparently opened a window or a door. The music was louder, the Glenn Miller arrangement of "A Nightingale Sang in Berkeley Square."

"I can work in a system just fine," Candy said.

"I imagine so," I said.

"So what's wrong with that?"

"Nothing."

We were quiet. The band on the roof was playing "Indian Summer." The smell of flowers seemed to have faded. The smell of Candy's perfume was stronger. My mouth was dry.

"Is dancing too systematic for you?" Candy said.

"No."

She got up and reached out toward me, and we began to dance, moving in a small circle on the narrow balcony, with the music drifting down. With her shoes off she was considerably smaller and her head reached only to my shoulder.

"Are you alone?" she said.

"Out here?"

"No, in your life."

"No. I am committed to a woman named Susan Silverman."

"Doesn't that cut down on your freedom?" Candy rested her head against my shoulder as we turned slowly in the darkness.

"Yes," I said. "But it's worth it."

"So you're not completely autonomous?"

"No."

"Good. It makes you easier to understand."

"Why do you need to understand me?" I said.

She took her right hand out of my left and slid it around to join her left hand at the small of my back. Unless I was willing to dance around with my left hand sticking out like a figure in a Roman fountain, I had nothing to do but put it around her. I did.

"I need to understand you so I can control you," Candy said.

"Your present technique is fairly effective," I said. My voice was hoarse. I cleared my throat slightly, trying not to make any noise. "For the short run."

"Throat a bit dry?" Candy said.

"That's just my Andy Devine impression," I said. "Sometimes I do Aldo Ray."

My throat felt tight, and there seemed to be more blood in my veins than I had begun the evening with. She giggled softly.

"Would you care to help me undress?" she said.

"Spenser's the name, helping's the game," I said. I sounded like Andy Devine with a cold. I could feel that old red obliterative surge I always felt at times like this. The band on the roof was playing "The Man I Love," featuring someone, not Lionel Hampton, on vibes.

"There are two buttons," Candy said. She took my hands in hers. "One here." We continued to move slowly with the music. "One here." She let the unbuttoned dress slide down her arms and drop to the floor behind her. There was moonlight amplified by some spillover from the hotel windows and the roof lighting. Her bra was the same plum color as her dress.

"Three snaps," she murmured. "Hooks and eyelets, actually, in a vertical line."

The bra slid down her arms in front of her and fell to the floor between us. "The panty hose while dancing will be a challenge," I whispered. I wasn't being secretive. It was the best I could talk.

"Try," she said. She stood almost still, her upper body moving slightly with the music. Her hands guided mine. It's hard to be graceful removing panty hose. We didn't fully succeed. But we got it done, and when I straightened, she wore only the gold around her neck. I felt oafishly overdressed.

"Now you," she said.

"Always hard to know what's best to do with a gun in this situation," I wheezed.

We were both naked finally, dancing on the balcony. The gun lay holstered on the table beside the cognac bottle. If an assassin broke in I could reach it in less than five minutes.

"What's that they're playing?" Candy said in my ear.

" 'I'll Never Smile Again,' " I said.

"I wish it were Ravel's 'Bolero,' " she said.

"At my age," I croaked, "you may have to settle for 'Song of the Volga Boatmen.' "

"Pick me up," she said. She was whispering now too. "Carry me to bed."

"Before I do," I said. "This is what it is. It leads nowhere. It means nothing more than the moment."

"I know. Pick me up. Carry me."

I did, she wasn't heavy. I snagged the gun, too, from the coffee table and took it with me when we went into the bedroom.

Chapter 10

WE WERE HAVING corned beef hash at Don Hernando's in the Beverly Wilshire. Candy had insisted that it was the world's best, and I was willing to let her think so. She had never breakfasted at R.D.'s Diner in South Glens Falls, New York.

Candy sipped her coffee. When she put the cup down, there was a lipstick imprint on the rim. Susan always did that too.

"Any guilt?" Candy said to me.

I ate a forkful of hash, took a small bite of toast, and chewed and swallowed. "I don't think so," I said.

"What about the woman you're committed to?"

"I'm still committed to her."

"Will you tell her?"

"Yes."

"Will she mind?"

"Not very much," I said.

"Would you mind if it were the other way?"

"Yes."

"Is that fair?"

"It's got nothing to do with fair," I said, "or unfair. I'm jealous. She's not. Perhaps it's a real recognition that hers would be an affair of the heart, while mine is of the flesh only, so to speak."

"My God, what a romantic distinction," Candy said. "So flowery too."

I nodded and drank some coffee.

"More than flowery," Candy said. "Victorian. Women make love, and men fuck."

"No need to generalize. We did more than fuck last night, but we're not in love. For Susan it wouldn't have to be love, but it would involve feelings that you and I don't have: interest, excitement, commitment, maybe some intrigue. For Suze it would involve relationship.

"I can't say for you, although I bet it had a little something to do with the agent you used to sleep with. For me it was sexual desire satisfied. I like you. I think you're beautiful. You seemed to be available. I guess we could say that what was involved for me was affectionate lust."

Candy smiled. "You talk well," she said. "And it's not the only thing."

"Aw, blush," I said.

"But if you tell—what's her name?"

"Susan."

"If you tell Susan, won't it make her a little unhappy to no good purpose?"

"It may make her a little unhappy, but the purpose is good."

"Easing your conscience?"

"Pop psych," I said.

"What do you mean?"

"The world's not that simple. I tell her because we should not have things we don't tell each other."

"Would you want to know?"

"Absolutely."

"And if you knew, would it be the end?"

"No. Dying is the only end for me and Suze."

"So you're not so all-fired wonderful. You don't risk that much by telling her."

"True," I said.

"But?"

"But what."

Candy's hash was barely nibbled. She poked at it with her fork.

"But there's more," she said. "I've oversimplified it again."

"Sure."

"Tell me."

"What difference does it make?" I said.

"I want to know," Candy said. "I've never met anyone like you. I want to know."

"Okay," I said. "I wouldn't do anything I couldn't tell her about."

"Are you ashamed of this?"

"No."

"Would you do something that would make you ashamed?"

"No."

She poked at her hash some more. "Jesus," she said. "I think you wouldn't. I've heard people say that before, but I never believed them. I don't think they even believed themselves. But you mean it."

"It's another way of being free."

"But how—"

I shook my head. "Eat your hash," I said. "We have a heavy crime-busting schedule. Let's fortify ourselves and not talk for a while." I ate more hash.

Candy opened her mouth and closed it and looked at me and then smiled and nodded. We ate our hash in silence. Then we paid the check, went out, got in Candy's MG, and drove to Century City.

Oceania Industries had executive offices high up in one of the towers. The waiting room had large oil paintings of Oceania's various enterprises: oil rigs, something that I took for a gypsum mine, a scene from a recent Summit picture, a long stand of huge pines. On the end tables were copies of the annual report and the several house organs from the various divisions. They had titles like *Gypsum Jottings* and *Timber Talk*.

There was no one in the reception room except a woman at a huge semicircular reception desk. Her fingernails were painted silver. She looked like Nina Foch.

"May I help you?" she said. Elegant. Generations of breeding.

I asked, "Are you Nina Foch?"

She said, "I beg your pardon?"

I said, "You left pictures for this?"

She said, "*May* I help you?" Stronger this time, but no less refined.

Candy gave her a card. "I'm with KNBS. I wonder if we might see Mr. Brewster."

"Do you have an appointment?" Nina said.

"No, but perhaps you could ask Mr. Brewster . . ."

Nina's eyes narrowed slightly. "I'm sorry," she said. "Mr. Brewster sees no one without an appointment."

"This is rather important," Candy said.

Nina looked even more severe, but patrician. "I'm sorry, miss, but there can be no exceptions. Mr. Brewster is—"

"Very busy," I said, ahead of her.

"Yes," she said. "He is, after all, the president of one of the largest corporations in the world."

I looked at Candy. "Gives you goose bumps, doesn't it," I said.

Candy placed her hands on the desk and leaned forward. She said to Nina Foch, "Some very disturbing charges have been leveled at Mr. Brewster. I should like, in the interests of fairness, to give him a chance to deny them before we go on the six o'clock news with the story."

Nina stared at us in a refined way for a moment and then got up abruptly and went through the big bleached-oak raised-panel door between the painting of the pine trees and the painting of the oil wells. In maybe three minutes she was back.

She sat behind her big circular reception desk and said, "Mr. Brewster will see you shortly." She didn't like saying it.

"Freedom of the press is a flaming sword," I said.

Candy looked at me blankly.

"Use it wisely," I said. "Hold it high. Guard it well."

"A. J. Liebling?" Candy said.

"Steve Wilson of *The Illustrated Press*. You're too young."

She shook her head again and did her giggle. "You really are goofy sometimes."

A tall man with platinum-blond hair and a developing stomach came into the reception room and hustled by us toward the bleached-oak door. His glen plaid suit fit well, but his shoes were shabby and the heels were turned. He went through the oak door and it closed behind him without sound.

Nina Foch was erect at her desk, without expression and apparently without occupation. She looked elegantly at the double doors that led out of the reception room to the ordinary corridor beyond.

A smallish man with a dimple in his chin and the look of a gymnast strode in through those double doors. Nina smiled at him. He nodded at her and did not look at us. He wore a Donegal tweed suit and a white shirt with a red bow tie. His shoes were tan pebble-grained brogues. He went through the oak door.

"Suit must itch like hell in California," I said to Candy. She smiled. Nina uncrossed her legs behind the desk and recrossed them the other way. She made an adjustment to the skirt hem.

A third man came in through the double doors. He nodded at Nina. Halfway across the room he stopped in front of the couch and looked at us. First at Candy. Then at me. Then at Candy again. He nodded. Then he looked at me again for a long time. He was a big guy, my size maybe, with longish hair styled back smoothly, the ears covered except where the lobes peeped out. He had on a good three-piece gray suit with a pink windowpane-plaid running through it. His aviator glasses were tinted amber. As he stood looking at us he had the suitcoat open and his hands on his hips. Truculent.

"Are you Grumpy, Sneezy, or Doc?" I said. Candy started to giggle and swallowed it.

"You, I know," he said, looking at Candy, hands still on his hips, the double-vent suitcoat flared out behind him. "You, I don't," he said to me. "Who are you?"

"I asked you first," I said.

"If I don't like you, you got troubles," he said.

"Aw, hell, I shoulda guessed. You're Grumpy."

Candy put her head down and her shoulders shook. It wasn't a giggle. She was laughing. Amber Glasses looked at me for another ten seconds, then turned and went through the door.

Candy's face was pink, and her eyes were bright when she looked at me. "Spenser," she said, "you're awful. Who do you suppose he was?"

"Security," I said. "I'll bet my album of Annette Funicello nudies on it."

"You made that up," Candy said.

"Wait and see," I said.

"No, I mean the part about Annette Funicello."

"Oh, yeah," I said. "But a man's only as good as his dream."

We waited perhaps five more minutes. Then a soft chime sounded at Nina Foch's desk. She picked up a white and gold phone that looked like it came from the Palace of Versailles. She listened and then put the phone down.

"You may go in now," she said. She didn't like saying that either.

The rug as we walked toward the door was deep enough to lose a dachshund in. I opened the door for Candy. It was hung so precisely that it seemed weightless. Candy took a deep breath.

I said, "I'm right beside you, babe."

She smiled and looked at me briefly and nodded. "I'm glad you are," she said. Then we walked through the door.

Chapter 11

WE WERE IN a room lined with bookshelves. There was leather furniture around and, on a round mahogany table in the middle of the room, a large globe. At the other end of the room was another door. It was open. The room beyond the open door seemed very bright. Candy preceded me. Sneezy, Grumpy, and Doc were sitting on a long couch to our right. The wall opposite the door was all glass, and the long green view of the L.A. Country Club below was a dazzler. In front of the wall, at right angles to the couch, was a desk about the size of Detroit. Behind it sat a man with large white teeth and dark hair flecked with gray. His face was deeply tanned. He wore a dark blue pin-striped suit with a vest that had lapels. His tie was an iridescent gray-blue tied in a small knot under a white pin-collar. He looked like the centerfold in *Fortune*.

He said, "You're Miss Sloan. I've seen you on the news. And your associate?"

Candy said, "Mr. Spenser."

"I'm Peter Brewster," he said. "This is Tom Turpin, our director of corporate public relations." He gestured at the guy with the glen plaid and the shabby shoes. "And Barrett Holmes, our legal counsel"—the gymnast with the dimpled chin. "And Rollie Simms. Mr. Simms is our director of corporate security." I grinned at Candy. "Since I understand you are about to level an accusation, I thought it would be prudent to have these gentlemen witness it. Barrett, if it's action-able, I'll want you to take steps immediately."

I said to the trio on the couch, "Excuse me, but which one of you three guys speaks no evil?"

Brewster gave me a basilisk stare.

He said, "I have very little time for humor."

I said, "But an awful lot of occasion."

He gave me that stare again.

Candy said, "Mr. Brewster, I have information that organized crime has infiltrated Summit Studios. Do you have any comment on that?"

"Shouldn't you take that question to Roger Hammond at Summit?"

"I have."

"And his response?"

"He had us put off studio property."

Brewster nodded. "The nature of your information?"

"I can't give you details, but I have an eyewitness."

"To what?"

"To a transaction involving Summit personnel and a member of the Los Angeles underworld."

"And the nature of that transaction?"

"A payoff."

Brewster nodded again. He looked at me.

"Is this your eyewitness?"

"No."

"Who is your eyewitness?"

Candy shook her head. "He'll have to remain anonymous for now."

"Of course," Brewster said. "Of course he would. You media types are all the same, aren't you. You have information but you can't give me specifics. You have an eyewitness, but he'll have to remain anonymous."

"Do you wish to comment on the allegations?" Candy said.

"The allegation is without foundation," Brewster said. "And you are without professional ethics. I shall be discussing you with the management of KNBS shortly."

"I'm only trying to do my job, Mr. Brewster," Candy said.

"And I seriously doubt that you'll have a job for very much longer," Brewster said.

"You mean, you're going to get me fired?" Candy's gaze was firm, but her voice had softened a little.

"Precisely," Brewster said.

I looked at Holmes, the lawyer. "Is that actionable?" I said.

"And I am sick of your smart mouth too," Brewster said. He did his stare again. "Who is your superior?"

"I have none," I said. "I'm not sure I even have an equal."

"Spenser," Candy said, "please! You're not helping. Do you have any statement for me, Mr. Brewster?"

"I've made it. Now I want you both off of Oceania property. Now."

Candy said, "Mr. Brewster—"

Brewster said, "Now."

Simms, the security type with the tinted glasses, got to his feet. I looked at him. "Simms," I said, "this horse's ass that you work for has made me very edgy. If you do anything more than stand up, I will put you in two weeks of traction."

Simms said, "Hey."

"I mean it," I said. "Sit down."

Candy's face was flushed. She moved in front of me. "Come on," she said. "You're making it worse. Come on. I want to go home."

Brewster pushed his desk intercom. "Miss Blaisdell," he said, "send some security people in here at once."

Candy said, "See what you've done. Come on, let's get out of here."

I said, "It is not dignified to run off like this."

"Come *on*," she said and headed for the door.

There was nothing left there for me to do. Telling Brewster he'd be hearing from me seemed graceless. I thought about kicking him, but by the time I got around the desk, the entire security force would be setting up gun emplacements in the reception room. I lingered another few seconds, hoping that Simms would lay hold of me. No luck. Nobody moved. Everyone looked at me. I felt like I'd stumbled into an Italian Western.

Candy was out the office door. She wasn't waiting. I was supposed to guard her. I went after her. On the way out I picked the globe off the table in the booklined room and dropped it on the floor. That oughta fix 'em.

Chapter 12

IN THE ELEVATOR there were tears in Candy's eyes. In the parking garage her lower lip was shaky. In her car, pulling out onto Santa Monica Boulevard, she cried.

As we passed Bedford Drive I said, "If you'll tell me why you're crying I'll buy you a large frappéed margarita at the Red Onion, and maybe a nacho supreme."

She sobbed. We crossed Camden.

I said, "It's down here, on Dayton at Beverly. You keep sobbing and driving and you'll miss an outstanding margarita."

She kept crying, but she turned right on Rodeo, drove down past stores that sold eight-hundred-dollar farmer's overalls, and parked near the corner of Dayton. Then she put her head down on the steering wheel and wept full out. I cranked the seat back as far as it would go on my side of the MG and leaned back and stretched my legs out and folded my arms on my chest and rested my head and closed my eyes and waited.

It took about five more minutes before she stopped. She straightened back in the seat, turned the rearview mirror toward her, and began to look at her face. Her breathing was still irregular, and a half sob caught her breath. She took makeup from her purse and began to readjust her face. I was still. When she got through she said, "Let's go."

We walked down to the Red Onion. Pink stucco, Mexicanesque tile, a bar on one side of the foyer and the dining room on the other. The bar was full of young women with very narrow backsides wearing very tight jeans with designer labels on the back pockets. They were talking with very young men with very narrow backsides wearing very tight jeans with designer labels on the back pockets.

We went to the dining room and each drank a margarita. Then we ordered two nacho supremes and another margarita. The waitress went away.

I said, "What happened at Oceania to make you cry?"

"They were so"—she shook her head—"they were so . . . mean."

"Nice guys work in the mailroom," I said.

She nodded. The waitress brought more margaritas.

"I know," Candy said. "I know that. I mean, it's the same in broadcasting. I know. But they were so—" She raised both hands slightly from the table, made a small open gesture, and let them drop.

"First of all why do you say 'they'? The three clucks on the couch barely spoke. Simms just made a few security-chief noises. How else would we know he was tough?"

"Well, it was really"—she twirled the stem of her glass—"it was really just him, I guess, and the rest of them looked threatening."

" 'Him' being Brewster?"

"Yes."

"He scared you by his talk of going to the station management?"

"No, not scared me. But . . ." She drank some of the margarita. It was a pale green. "A station manager is quite often friends with big shots in town. I mean, they really can make waves when the license comes up for renewal, or when they talk with other big shots about where they advertise."

"You could get fired?"

"Well, it's possible. Or not get more money or not get good assignments. Get a troublemaker reputation —first Hammond, and now Brewster complaining to the station."

"That made you cry?"

"Not just that."

"What else?"

"Well, I was alone and they were all there."

"Well, you weren't absolutely, completely, one hundred percent alone," I said.

"You were making it worse."

"Admitted. I have trouble keeping my mouth shut in boardrooms and penthouses and executive suites and stuff. It's a bad habit. But I was still on your side. You weren't alone."

"You're a man," she said.

I had been leaning forward with my elbows on the table. I sat back and put my hands in my lap.

"Jesus Christ," I said.

"I was alone in there with five men, four of them actively hostile. It's very hard. You don't know what that's like. He dismissed me like I was a beetle. A bug. Nothing. 'Get out,' he said, 'I'm going to speak to your boss.'"

"Jesus."

"And my boss will say, 'Sure, Pete, old pal, she's a pushy broad. I'll let her go.'"

I took one hand out of my lap and rubbed the lower part of my face with it. The nacho supremes came. We ordered two bottles of Dos Equis beer.

"Okay," I said. "You're afraid for your job."

Her eyes were filling again. "The only woman," she said.

"*Only* woman is true," I said. "*Alone* is not true."

"You wouldn't understand."

Suze, where are you when I need you. "Talk a little more," I said. "Maybe I will."

— 78 —

"You weren't *with* me. You were there to *protect* me."

"Ah-hah," I said.

She looked at me. There was no humor in her look. Her eyes were wet and her face was somber. "What's that mean?" she asked.

"It means, loosely, oh-oh. It means that since I've been with you, you've been between Scylla and Charybdis. You need me to protect you, but the need compromises your sense of self."

"It underscores female dependency."

"And in the office up there, you were scared. And being scared, you were glad I was with you, and that underscored the female dependency even more."

She shrugged.

"And when you told me you could get information from an agent you used to sleep with, you weren't showing off your liberation, you were being bitter. You were trying to make light of your feeling that to get what you needed, you had to go to a man and get an I.O.U. in return for sexual favors, or something like that."

She poked at her food with her fork, and ate a small bite. The nacho was about the size of a bluefin tuna. When they said supreme, they meant supreme.

"Something like that. You misunderstood."

"Yes, I did. Now I don't."

"Maybe."

I finished my beer.

Candy smiled at me a little. "Look," she said. "You're a good guy. I know you care about me, but you're a white male, you can't understand a minority situation. It's not your fault."

I gestured at the waitress for another beer. Candy hadn't touched hers. Appalling.

While I waited for the beer, I worked on the nacho. When the beer came, I drank about a quarter of it and said to Candy, "Extend that logic, and we eventually have to decide that no one can understand anyone. Maybe the matter of understanding has been over-rated. Maybe I don't have to understand your situation to sympathize with it, to help you alter it, to be on your side. I've never experienced starvation either, but I'm opposed to it. When I encounter it, I try to alleviate it. I sympathize with its victims. The question of whether I understand it doesn't arise."

She shook her head. "That's different," she said.

"Maybe it isn't. Maybe civilization is possible, if at all, only because people can care about conditions they haven't experienced. Maybe you need understanding like a fish needs a bicycle."

"You're quite thoughtful," she said, "for a man your size."

"You never been my size," I said. "You wouldn't understand."

Chapter 13

THE COPS FOUND Mickey Rafferty lying in the open door of his room at the Marmont with his feet sticking out into the hall and three bullets in his chest. Someone had heard shots and called the cops. But no one had seen anything and no one knew anything.

Candy and I got this from a cop named Samuelson in the empty studio where, mornings from nine to ten, a talk show called *New Day L.A.* bubbled and frothed. It was four fifty in the afternoon. Candy had some news to read at six.

"We found him this morning," Samuelson said, "about twelve hours ago. We talked to some people at the studio. They said he was close to you."

Candy's face was pale and blank. She sat on a sofa on the set, her legs crossed, her hands in her lap. She nodded.

"I'm sorry to be the one to tell you," Samuelson said.

Candy nodded again. Samuelson was sitting on one corner of the anchor desk, his arms folded. He was square-faced and nearly bald, with a large drooping mustache and tinted glasses in gold frames.

"Way I figure it happened," he said, "someone knocked on the door, and when he opened it, they shot him in the chest."

Candy shook her head with little rapid movements, almost as if she were shivering.

"You got anything else?" I said.

"Not so far," Samuelson said. He was chewing gum and occasionally cracked it. "Hoping maybe Miss Sloan would be able to help us."

Candy shook her head. "I don't know anything," she said. "I don't have any idea why someone would want to kill Mickey."

"How about you, Boston?" Samuelson popped his gum at me.

"No," I said, "I only met him once."

"I know this is a tough time to talk about it, Miss Sloan," Samuelson said. "But I would like to talk some more when you can. Maybe tomorrow?"

Candy nodded.

"Maybe you could come downtown," Samuelson said. "Tomorrow, maybe around two in the afternoon, say." He took his wallet out, slipped a card from it, and gave it to Candy. "If you can't make it then, give us a call, and we'll arrange a better time."

Candy took the card.

Samuelson looked at me. "Wouldn't it be a coincidence if Rafferty getting burned had something to do with this investigation you're helping with, Boston."

I shrugged.

"If it turned out that way, you'd get in touch with us right away, wouldn't you, Boston." He gave me a card too.

"It's every citizen's duty," I said.

"Yeah, okay." Samuelson unfolded from the anchor desk. He was tall and looked in shape, not heavy, but like a tennis player or a swimmer. He moved smoothly.

"I'll be looking for you tomorrow, Miss Sloan. You come too, Boston," he said.

Candy said yes, not very loud. And Samuelson went out of the studio. It was dead quiet. The weighted studio door swung shut. Candy got up from the couch and walked over to it and looked out through the small double-glass window. Then she walked back over and stood beside me.

"They killed him," she said.

"I gather we're not telling the cops everything we know?" I said.

"They killed Mickey," Candy said. "Doesn't that—" She spread her hands.

"There are all kinds of things it does," I said. "But trying to talk about it is inadequate. If *they* did kill him and *they* are the same people that had you beat up, then it says they are in earnest."

"You mean they might try to kill me?"

"They might. But I won't let them."

Candy turned and walked away, across the empty studio, stepping carefully over the lash of cables on the floors, and on the far side of the studio, she stopped, turned back, leaned her arms on a camera, and put one foot up on the bumper ring that went around the lower end of the dolly.

"You think you are very tough, don't you. People die, people are hurt. You're matter-of-fact about it, aren't you. 'They might try to kill you, girlie, but don't worry about it. I'll take care of you. Big strong me.' Well, what if they kill *you*. You ever think of that?"

"No more than I have to," I said.

"Wouldn't be manly, would it."

"Wouldn't do any good," I said.

She stared at me over the body of the camera.

"What'll we do, Spenser?" she said. "What in hell will we do?"

"Some of it you have to decide," I said. "Maybe you have already. For instance what do we tell Samuelson and how much? A few minutes ago you told him nothing. You going to stick with that?"

"Should I?"

"Not my decision," I said.

"I'm afraid, if they know, they'll get involved in the whole deal and everyone will shut up and I won't get a story."

"Or they might dig it out and clean it up," I said. "They can do that sometimes."

"But it would be them, not me. I want this. I don't want a bunch of cops getting it."

"If the cops are involved, there's not much reason for the bad guys to harm you anymore," I said. "Their whole point is to keep you from the cops."

"I need this story," she said.

"Okay," I said, "but don't think Samuelson is going to be easy. Cops hate coincidence. You've employed a detective from Boston for an unspecified investigation, and then your boyfriend gets killed."

"He's not my boyfriend. Wasn't."

"That's not the point. He was perceived as such. Samuelson isn't going to be happy with the hypothesis that there's no connection."

"That's his problem," Candy said. She was resting her chin on her folded arms, staring across the barrel of the camera, past me, at the blank off-white curtain that backdropped part of the set.

"He's being nice with you, and careful, because you're in the media, and he knows you can cause him aggravation. But cops have a high aggravation tolerance, and if he has to, he'll take the weight, as the saying goes. Then he can become your problem . . . and mine."

"I suppose it could be trouble for you."

"Suppressing evidence. Cops—and D.A.'s and judges —disapprove of it generally."

"You can go back to Boston."

"While you do what?"

"I need this story." She wasn't gazing at the off-white backdrop now. She was looking at me.

— 84 —

"Like the cops," I said, "the bad guys walk a little more carefully around you than they might someone else. Killing a reporter makes a lot of waves. Remember the reporter that got blown up in Arizona?"

She nodded.

"So do they, and maybe they won't kill you if they don't have to. But if you're running around making more waves than you'd make dead, then the logic seems inescapable."

"That means you think I should tell the police?"

"No," I said. "That means I'll stay."

Chapter 14

THAT NIGHT THERE was no dancing on the balcony. We ate a room-service dinner in near perfect silence and went to bed early. What a difference a day makes. I lay on the bed in my room and watched an Angels game on television until I got tired. Then I switched everything off and went to bed. Sleep. Death's second self.

In the morning we went to Candy's apartment to check her mail and listen to her phone-answering machine and get some clean clothes. The sun was bright off the pool and filled the room. There was a breeze. The faint movement of the pool made the light glance and quiver. Candy stood by her desk in the living room sorting through her mail. She had on a dark blue suit with gold piping. She punched on the phone recorder as she looked at the mail, and Mickey Rafferty's voice came up.

"Candy," it said, "where the hell are you? I've been trying to get you all day. I braced Felton and I know he's scared. All we have to do is keep on the pressure, and he'll crack. I'll keep calling till I get you. . . . I love you, babe."

Candy dropped the mail and slowly sank to her knees and put her arms around herself and began to rock slightly back and forth, sitting on her heels, her head hanging. I stepped over and shut off the recorder.

Candy murmured something.

I said, "What?" and bent over to hear her.

She said, "A voice from the grave," and gave a little snicker. "From the other side, through the magic of machines." She snickered again. And then she was still and rocked.

I squatted beside her on the floor and said, "Would you care for a hug or a comforting pat, or would that make it worse?"

She shook her head, but I didn't know if she was saying no to the hug or no, it wouldn't make it worse. So I stayed where I was and did nothing, which I probably ought to do more of, and after a while she stopped rocking and put a hand on my thigh to steady herself and then stood up. I stood with her.

"Poor little Mickey," she said. "He acted so tough."

"He was tough," I said. "He was just small."

"Big or small," she said, "bullets would have killed him anyway."

The rest of the phone recordings had to be listened to. I was thinking how to go about it.

"If I'd been a weathergirl," Candy said, "Mickey'd be alive."

"You've had a bad time. You're entitled to be silly," I said. "But don't do it too much. You know his dying wasn't your fault."

"Whose fault was it?"

"I guess most of the blame resides with the guy who burned him. I'd guess old fat Franco. A little of the blame is Mickey's. He screwed around with stuff he didn't know about. It's a way to get hurt."

"Franco?"

"Yeah, the fat guy that beat you up. His name's Franco."

"How do you know that?"

"Learned from the blond guy I talked with at the Farmers Market."

"And you think he killed Mickey?"

"You talked to Felton and got beat up by Franco.

— 87 —

Mickey talked to Felton and got shot. Wouldn't you guess Franco?"

"Yes."

"That would seem the handle to all of this," I said. "Old Franco."

"Handle?"

"Yeah. We've spent all this time talking to people on whom we have nothing. We've already got Franco for kidnapping and assault. He's probably hired help. So he has no reason to cover up for his employers if it costs him."

"I guess that's so. But he's not the one I want," Candy said. She was starting to concentrate. The shock was receding.

"Not finally," I said. "But to get any tangle straightened out you have to find one end of the rope. Franco's one end."

"Okay." Candy was frowning with interest. "Okay. I'll buy that. Now the problem is to find him." She was drumming her fingers softly against her thigh. "You have any thoughts on that?"

"How did you find him?" I said.

"I didn't. He found me."

"And Mickey?"

"I see. He found Mickey too. I'd talked to Felton, and Franco showed up. Mickey talked to Felton and, we assume, Franco showed up again. Are you saying I should talk to Felton again and make a target of myself?"

"You or me."

"It shouldn't be you," Candy said. "Mickey wasn't your friend. You didn't come out here to be a, what, a—"

"Sitting duck, clay pigeon, sacrificial lamb."

She nodded. "Any of those. No. It's my job."

"Okay," I said.

"No big macho talk about 'man's work'?"

"Nope. In fact it makes no difference. I do it, and I have to protect me and you. You do it, and I have to protect you and me."

She stopped drumming her fingers and looked at me without expression for a moment. "Yes," she said. She looked at me some more. "Yes, that's true. I may not like it, but it's the way it is. You can protect me a lot better than I can protect myself. I want to do it."

"Yeah," I said. "I thought you would."

She walked to the glass doors and stared out at her blue pool. Her fingers were drumming again on her thigh.

"You know, I've lived in this house three years and I'll bet I've been in the damn pool twice."

"When this is over," I said, "we'll have a victory swim."

"When it's over," she said. Her back was still to me. "Christ, I wish it were over a long time ago."

I was quiet.

"When I first came up with this story and started on it, I was so excited. Celebrity, advancement, money." She shook her head and stared out at the pool. "Now I wish it were done. Now I have to finish it, and all it does is scare me."

"There's no business like show business," I said.

She turned from the window. "Maybe," she said, "I'd better learn to use that gun."

I went out to her car and got it out of the glove compartment and brought it back into her living room. She looked at it without affection. I pressed the release button and dropped the clip out. Then I ran the receiver back and popped a shell out of the chamber.

"Had a round chambered," I said.

"If you're going to teach me anything," Candy said, "you'll have to speak a language I understand."

"Sure. I just mean he had a bullet up in the chamber,

ready to fire. Usually you would leave it in the magazine till you were ready to shoot. Safer that way."

"Are you saying, when they trailed us into the Farmers Market, they were ready to shoot us?"

"Maybe, or maybe they were careless and stupid."

"Is it loaded now?"

"No. Try it out."

She snapped the empty gun several times, aiming at the far wall. "The trigger's not hard to pull," she said.

"Not the way you mean," I said.

"You mean, it's hard to shoot someone?"

"Can be."

"Is this all I do, point it and shoot?"

"If it's loaded and cocked, yes."

"Show me how to load it."

I showed her how to slide the magazine into the handle.

"It's heavier with the bullets," she said.

"A little," I said.

"If I pull the trigger now, will it go off?"

"No. You've got to jack a round up into the chamber. Look." I showed her how. "Now if you pull the trigger it will shoot." I took it from her and took out the clip and ejected the chambered bullet and pulled the trigger. The hammer fell with an empty click. Then I handed her the pistol.

"Okay, you do it."

She put the magazine in, ran the action back, and looked at me. "Now I can shoot."

"Yes."

"Do I have to push the thing back every time I shoot?"

"No. Only the first time. Then it does it by itself. After the first time you just keep squeezing the trigger. When it's empty, the breech will lock open."

"What if I need more than, what is it, six shots?"

"Yes. If you do, you can reload the magazine. But if you've fired six rounds and need more, you probably won't have time to reload. I advise flight."

She practiced loading and cocking a couple of times. Then she pointed the empty gun and practiced a couple of clicks. "Am I doing it right?" she said.

"Yeah. Try to shoot from close. Don't waste time on shooting from very far. The gun's not made for it, and neither are you. Shoot for the middle of the body. It allows the most margin of error. You might want to shoot with both hands, like this." I showed her. "Or if it's sort of a far shot, you might do it like this." I showed her the target-shooting stance and told her how to let out the air, and not breathe, and squeeze the trigger. "All of that is unlikely," I said. "What you'll want to hit with the gun, if you need to, will probably be very close up and hard to miss. What you need to do most of all is remember you've got it, and be willing to use it. Keep in mind that they want to kill you."

"You've shot people?"

"Yes."

"Is it awful?"

"No. It's fashionable to say so, but no. It's not awful. Often it's fairly easy. Not messy like stabbing or clubbing or strangling, that sort of thing. It's relatively impersonal. Click. Bang. Dead."

"Don't you mind?"

"Yes, I mind. I don't do it if I don't have to. But I've never shot anyone when it wouldn't have been a lot worse not to. "

"Do you remember the first time?"

"The time, not the person. It was in Korea. He was just a shape on a night patrol."

"And it didn't bother you?"

"Not as much as it would have if he'd shot me."

"It's always in context for you, isn't it?"

"What? Right and wrong?"

"Yes."

"Yes."

"Isn't that ethical relativism?"

"I think so," I said. "Can you shoot if you have to?"

"Yes," Candy said. "I believe I can."

Chapter 15

WE WENT DOWN to the hall of justice the next afternoon and spent an hour and a half explaining to
Samuelson that our investigation of the moving picture business had nothing to do with Mickey Rafferty's
death. I don't think Samuelson believed it, but there
was nothing much that he could do about it, and he
knew it and he knew we knew it so he ushered us
out after an hour and a half with a fair amount of
grace. Candy drove us up over what was left of Bunker
Hill and down to Fifth Street and then to Figueroa
and then onto Wilshire.

"I know it's dumb," I said, "but I kind of like downtown L.A."

"You do?"

"Yeah. It feels more like a city is supposed to."

"I never come down here except for a story, but I
don't really like cities."

"You're in the right place," I said.

We drove west on Wilshire past the big old Ambas-
sador Hotel with its brown stucco cottages. Bobby
Kennedy had been shot there, on the way out of the
ballroom, after a speech.

"I know Felton's home address," Candy said. "The
first time I saw him, I went to his home."

"Want to cruise on up there and see if he's home?"

"Yes," Candy said. "If he isn't, we'll wait."

I looked at my watch. Four thirty. "Maybe we

should stop someplace and get a few sandwiches to go. In case it's a long wait."

She nodded. In Beverly Hills we stopped at something that appeared to be a French delicatessen. I went in and bought cheese and bread and country pâté and an apple and a pear and a bottle of red wine. They put all this in a paper bag that had a straw-basket design printed on the side, and I took it out, slipped it into the trunk, and got back into the passenger's side beside Candy.

"We're armed and provisioned, baby. Let's roll."

We turned up Beverly Drive, heading north toward the hills. Candy was quiet as she drove. Across Santa Monica I looked at the houses. They were close together and quite near the street, but looking down the driveways and peering around shrubs as we went past, I could see the depth of the lot. Ample room for pools and tennis courts and hot tubs and patios and croquet lawns.

"What do you call the place where croquet is played?" I said to Candy.

"Excuse me?"

"Is it a croquet field or a croquet court or what?"

"I don't know."

"My God, next thing you'll tell me you don't play polo."

She shook her head. I looked at the houses some more. They were often Spanish with a touch of Tudor. They frequently had both wood and stone siding, and the small lawns in front were consistently well tended. Palm trees were metronomically regular in their spacing and identity along the narrow border between the sidewalk and the street. And nothing moved. It looked like an empty set. No dogs sitting in the front yards with their tongues out looking at pedestrians. No cats. No children. No bicycles. No basketball rims on garages. No baseballs, tree huts. No squirrels.

"Place looks like Disneyland after hours," I said to Candy. "Deserted."

"Oh, yes. It always is."

"What are they doing in there," I said, "watching a videotape of people living?"

Candy smiled but not like she enjoyed it. "I guess so," she said. "I never thought much about it."

We crossed Sunset. The Hills began.

"That mansion still here on Sunset where the guy painted explicit genitals on the nude statues out front?"

Candy nodded.

"A realist," I said.

"Spenser," Candy said, "I just don't feel like making amusing conversation right now, okay? My friend is dead. I may be dead soon. I'm scared and sad and I don't see how you can talk about nonsense as if nothing had happened."

"I could keen," I said.

She frowned. "Keen?"

"You know, as in 'keening and wailing and gnashing of teeth.' "

"You know you're probably being cheery, but please don't joke now. Let's just be quiet."

"How about I just gnash a little bit. Very softly. You'll barely hear me."

She smiled slightly.

I said, very softly, "Gnash."

She smiled more and her shoulders shook slightly. "Gnash."

She laughed. "Okay. Okay. You are, in fact, as loony as I thought you were. We're setting ourselves up like two worms on a hook, and you're riding around saying 'Gnash.' "

We swung off Beverly Drive and into Coldwater Canyon. The road was steeper now, and when we swung onto Linda Crest, we began going up steeply in a series of reverse curves. Candy shifted up and down as the MG hugged the turns.

"This is what it was born for," I said.

"This car? Yes. It's always fun to drive it up here. I always feel like Mario Andretti or somebody."

"Better looking though."

"Thank you."

Sam Felton's house was the last one on the street. Beyond it the hills terraced back down toward L.A., and the city spread out below it. There was a stucco wall with an iron gate in it. When we rang, a voice came out of a small speaker in one of the gateposts.

"Who's calling, please?" it said.

"Candy Sloan to see Mr. Felton."

"Mr. Felton is not home now. Would you leave a message?"

"We'd prefer to come in and wait," Candy said.

"I'm sorry, that isn't possible. I don't know when Mr. Felton will be home. If you'll leave a message, I'm sure he'll be in touch."

"No thanks," Candy said. A small sign beside the speaker said PROTECTED BY THE BEL-AIR PATROL. "We'll wait."

There was a click from the speaker and then silence. Candy shrugged. "He'll have to come in or go out sometime," Candy said.

"Back way?" I said.

"Not in these hills," Candy said. "You'd have to drive over someone's roof."

I nodded. We waited. We ate our picnic. At ten of seven a dark green BMW sedan drove into a turn in front of Felton's house and stopped. A man peered out at us through the front windshield.

"Felton," Candy said.

He got out of the car and waddled toward us. "Something I can do for you?" he said.

"Mr. Felton, it's Candy Sloan, KNBS, remember? I spoke with you before about movie racketeering."

"I remember. I thought that was finished."

"There's been some new developments, Mr. Felton. I'll need to discuss them with you before we broadcast them."

"I don't believe I know this gentleman," Felton said.

"Mr. Spenser is helping me with the investigation," Candy said.

Felton nodded at me. I said, "Glad to meet you."

Felton looked at the gate and then looked at us and then looked at his car. If he opened the gate to go in, would we go in with him? It would be embarrassing to get back in the car and drive away. Could he stall till the Bel-Air Patrol galloped by? He looked at me again. There was nothing he could do with me. I was twenty years younger and four inches taller. He opted for dignity.

"Come on in," he said. "We'll have a drink and I'll tell you what I can."

"Thank you," Candy said.

Felton unlocked the gate with a key that hung on a retractable key chain, attached to a clip on a big wide Western-style belt. He had a large stomach, and the belt was cinched right across the middle so that there was an unseemly bulge both above and below the belt. The belt held up some brand-new baggy jeans and was supplemented by wide red suspenders. Glamorous. He had on a white collarless shirt with a pleated front. His hair was shoulder length. On his feet were sandals. No socks. He held the gate open, and we went through and preceded him up the path. At the front door he used a different key, and then we were inside.

The house was cool, elegant, and expansive, gleaming with brass and ebony, filled with Oriental objets d'art, with parqueted and marble floors and floor-to-ceiling windows providing a view from almost every room.

An aging Mexican woman in a green housedress and a white apron appeared in the foyer. She stood quietly by an arched entry that appeared to lead into a dining room.

"What will you drink?" Felton asked us.

"White wine," Candy said.

"Beer," I said.

Felton spoke to the woman in Spanish. She smiled and disappeared.

"Come on in the living room," Felton said. "We can get comfortable and then we can talk."

There was an enormous black marble fireplace in the far wall of the living room. On either side were French doors, thinly curtained, through whose translucence the lights of Los Angeles glittered in the gathering evening.

Candy and I sat together on a huge white couch highlighted with bright green satin casual pillows. I tucked two behind me to keep from sinking into the quagmire of cushions. The Mexican woman brought in a large silver tray. On it were a glass of white wine and a bottle of Carta Blanca beer and a glass, and what I took to be a glass of tequila on a saucer with a wedge of lime and a small dish of salt with a silver spoon beside it. She placed the tray on a low glass coffee table and smiled and left.

I poured my beer. Felton picked up the lime wedge, sucked on it, put a little salt on his hand, drank the tequila and lapped the salt. He smiled. "The only way to go," he said. Jolly.

Candy sipped her wine. I drank some beer.

Felton said, "If you'll excuse me, I'll wash my hands and then we can talk."

Candy said, "Of course."

Felton left the room. The Mexican woman came back in with a fresh glass of tequila and a fresh lime and smiled at us and left.

The room was still. There were Oriental rugs on the floor. Opposite me, on a tapestry that ran from floor-to-ceiling, an Oriental warrior on a horse gazed into a distant valley where peasants worked fields with water buffalo. My beer was gone. Would the Mexican woman know without being told? Would she simply appear without a sign? No. No one appeared.

"Do you suppose he's run off," Candy said.

I shrugged. Candy drank some wine. Then Felton came back. He kicked off his sandals, picked up his second tequila, and polished it off with some more lime and salt. Then he sat cross-legged on another large white couch across from us. The Mexican woman appeared in the door. Felton spoke again in Spanish, and she disappeared.

"Now," he said, "how can I help?" He leaned forward slightly. It was as far as he could, and rested his elbows on his thighs. The Mexican woman brought me another beer and Felton another tequila.

Candy said, "Do you know Mickey Rafferty?"

There was a bowl of popcorn on an end table beside Felton. He took a handful. "Rafferty," he said and put some popcorn in his mouth. He chewed the popcorn. "Sure," he said, "doesn't he do stunt work?"

"Not anymore," Candy said. "He's dead."

"Oh, my God. Really? What happened. Was it a stunt?"

"No," Candy said, "he was shot to death in his room at the Marmont."

Felton raised his eyebrows and formed a silent *wow* with his lips.

We were quiet. Felton ate some more popcorn. He

ate rapidly, taking a handful and pushing it all into his mouth with his flattened palm. He drank his tequila.

"Isn't that terrible," he said. "Isn't that terrible. Awful."

"Can you tell us anything about it?" Candy said.

Felton's upper lip looked a little moist. It might have been tequila. But it might have been sweat. He ate some more popcorn.

"How on earth could I tell you anything?"

"I have information," Candy said, "that you were the last person he saw before he died."

There was a little moisture now on Felton's forehead. It wasn't tequila. He looked at his watch.

"That's insane. I barely knew him. I hadn't seen him for weeks. I wouldn't remember if I had seen him. I've never had two words with him."

I thought about him looking at his watch.

"No," Candy said. "I know better."

I thought about him leaving after we got here to wash his hands.

"Now listen, Candy, I know you think I'm involved in some crazy shakedown, but this is going too far. I'm willing to help. I know you've got a job to do. But . . ." He gestured futilely with both hands.

I slid my gun out of the hip holster and held it in my right hand down between the couch cushion and the arm of the couch. Felton didn't see me. He looked at his empty tequila glass. Then he looked toward the front hall.

"I mean are you saying I killed him?"

Candy had no expression on her face. She stared straight at Felton.

"You probably didn't kill him," she said. "Did you have it done?"

Felton slapped both hands palm down on the tops of his thighs. "For God's sake, that's enough," he said.

Candy continued to look at him. I continued to keep the gun concealed down between the cushions. Felton looked toward the front hall again and his hopes were realized. Franco had arrived.

Chapter 16

HE WAS DEFINITELY fat, probably two hundred and fifty on a frame no more than five feet nine. On the other hand Vasili Alexeyev is fat too. The thought was not comforting. Franco was balding and he hadn't fought it. What was left was cut very short, so that he seemed to be balder than he was. The Vandyke was black and so was the mustache. He was wearing a flowered shirt and green knit slacks and dark brown moccasins. The shirt hung outside the pants. Probably to hide a gun. Or maybe he thought it was elegant. I looked at Candy. Her face was frozen, without expression. She looked at Franco and was perfectly still.

Behind Franco was the blond charmer I had rousted in the parking lot at the Farmers Market. He'd never wear a flowered shirt. He wouldn't let it hang outside. He'd hide his gun in a shoulder rig under an unstructured linen jacket with the collar turned up.

I looked at Felton. It was as if he didn't have to pretend anymore and his glands could relax. His face was now shiny with sweat, and some had beaded on his upper lip. His expression was a mixture of gratitude and terror.

Franco looked at Candy and said, "Well, well, newsbirdie. You thought I didn't mean it last time?"

Candy was quiet. There was a faint sense of a foreign accent in Franco's voice, too dim to identify, merely the echo of a distant birth.

"Huh?" he said. "Did you think I didn't mean it?"

"I thought you meant it," Candy said.

"Then what are you doing here, birdie, huh? If you thought I meant it, what are you doing here?"

"My job," Candy said. There was no affect in her voice.

Franco looked at his helper. "How about that, Bubba. Her job, you hear that? She's doing her fucking job. Huh? You like that, Bubba?"

"Yeah," Bubba said. "Yeah, that's good."

Felton said, "What are you going to do, Franco?"

Franco looked at him for a moment and shook his head. "Look at the sweat," he said. "Give fat a bad name, guys like you."

Felton wiped his hand over his face. "Well, what're you?" he said.

"You called us," Franco said. "What'd you have in mind?"

"They were talking about me killing Rafferty," Felton said.

Franco made a sound between a grunt and a laugh. "You ain't got the 'nads to kill anything, except maybe a quart of tequila," he said. Then he looked at Candy and said, "Come on, you and your date take a ride with us."

Candy looked at me. I said "Nope."

Franco looked at me for the first time. "I wasn't asking," he said. "Get moving, huh?"

I said "Nope" again. It had a nice rhythm to it.

Bubba had moved a little to Franco's right, but neither showed a weapon yet. That's one of the mistakes tough guys make. They overrate how tough they are. They aren't careful.

I took the gun out from the cushions and pointed it at them. No harm in being careful. I said "Nope."

Franco and Bubba looked at the gun. So did Felton.

His face got sweatier. Candy didn't move. She seemed inside a kind of deep stillness.

"We have here," I said to Candy, "persuasive evidence of complicity between Felton and Franco, and of course the legendary Bubba. Bubba is on hourly wage, I suspect, and doesn't count for much. But I think we could make something pretty good out of Franco and old Sammy."

"What can we really prove?" Candy said.

"We can prove Franco beat you up. We can prove when we came here to talk with Sam Felton about Mickey, he called Franco, and Franco came and attempted to remove us. The threat of force was clearly implied."

"I want it all," Candy said.

"Cops can get it all if we give them this," I said. "Old Sam here will melt like butter on a flapjack when Samuelson gets him down to the Hall of Justice. So would Bubba, but he probably doesn't know anything."

"Don't get to feeling too good about that gun, huh?" Franco said. "I seen guns before. It ain't going to buy you all that much."

"If you do anything incautious," I said, "it can buy you the farm."

Candy seemed not even to hear Franco. She barely heard me. She was way inside somewhere. "I want it all," she said again. "I want to get it myself."

"You've got enough," I said. "You've broken it, let the cops clean up. They're good at it. They've got the personpower for it."

She didn't even smile at "personpower." No one else did either. No accounting for people's sense of humor. She was looking right at Franco now. "Did you shoot Mickey?" she said.

Franco made a small grin. "Sure," he said.

— 104 —

"You shot him?"

"Yes. I just said so, huh?"

Bubba edged slightly more to the right.

I said, "Don't do that, Bubba. I'm good with this. I'll drop you where you stand."

Franco said, "And while you're shooting him, what do you think I'll be doing, huh?"

I said, "I can drop him and you before you can clear the piece. You made one mistake coming in here with your hands empty. Don't make another one."

Candy said, "You can't shoot him, Spenser. He's our key to the whole story."

I said, "Yes, I can. We've still got Felton," and then everything went to hell. The Mexican woman walked in through the archway and stopped next to Franco when she saw the gun. Franco stepped behind her. I raised my gun. Candy said "No," and pushed at my arm. Franco was around the corner of the archway. Bubba had his gun out. I yanked my arm free of Candy and shot Bubba twice and shoved Candy down on the sofa and sprawled over her facing the archway. The Mexican woman was crouched on the floor near the archway. Felton was still cross-legged on the opposite couch, body bent as close to double as he could get, both hands over his head. Bubba had fallen backward to the floor. The smell of gunshot was in the room but no sound. The hum of central air conditioning filled an otherwise soundless void. Candy was motionless beneath me.

Then Franco's voice came from behind the archway. "Come on, Felton," Franco said. "Get off the couch and walk over here."

Felton kept his hands clutched over his head and looked up in my direction.

"Come on," Franco said again. "He won't shoot. He needs you alive, don't you, boyfriend. You kill him and you got nothing. Besides, I can blast the Mex from here and not even move. So we'll trade. Felton walks and you get the Mex, huh?"

I didn't say anything. I kept the gun on the entryway. I took a quick check on Felton from the corner of my eye. I didn't think he was a threat, but I hadn't counted on the Mexican woman either.

Franco said, "Get your fat ass out here, Felton, and now. Or you want to stay with them?"

"No," Felton said. His voice was squeaky. "No. I'm coming." He got off the couch and scurried fatly over to the archway and through.

Franco said, "We're leaving now, boyfriend. I'm backing out behind Felton. He's fat enough even for me. You have to kill him, huh? To get to me. Then what you got?"

I didn't speak. I could hear Candy's breath coming a little short beneath me. I could smell her perfume too, now that the shooting fumes were beginning to thin. I heard shuffling sounds recede down the front hall, then the front door opened and closed. I didn't move. Franco could open the front door and shut it without leaving, and when I came charging through the archway, he could cut me in half.

Candy said in a muffled voice, "You're smothering me."

I eased off of her and stood out of line of the archway, beside the couch.

Candy said, "Have they gone?"

I put my finger on my mouth and shook my head. "I guess so," I said loud enough for Franco to hear me. I moved over beside the archway and waited. The Mexican woman crouched where she had been. Candy stayed down on the couch. Then I heard the front door open again and shut. And silence. A double fake? Faintly I heard a car door slam. No double fake. I rolled around the corner of the archway in a crouch.

Franco could have sent Felton out to start the car. The hall was empty. I opened the front door and watched the taillights of a car disappear up the street. I went back into the living room.

With considerable emphasis I said, "Son of a bitch."

"I shouldn't have hit your arm," Candy said.

"True. But you didn't have much chance to think." I was looking down at Bubba. There was blood on his chest and his eyes were wide and silent.

"I was afraid I'd lose the story," she said.

"I know." No more hanging out at Venice Beach, Bubba. No more pumping iron. No more suntan oil and choker bathing suits.

"But I risked your life for it," Candy said.

"Part of the job description," I said. The Mexican woman was standing against the wall by the archway watching us.

"And now we've lost Sam Felton."

I nodded. The Mexican woman watched everything I did. Her eyes fixed on my face. I said to Candy, "We've got to tell the cops."

"No."

"Yes. I've killed a guy in front of a witness. There's no way out." I looked at the Mexican woman. "Do you speak English, ma'am?" I said.

"No speak," she said. *"Español."*

"See," Candy said. "She doesn't even understand English. She'll never even call the police."

"She says she doesn't speak English," I said. "That doesn't mean she doesn't. It doesn't mean she hasn't friends who speak English. It doesn't mean that the L.A.P.D. doesn't have Spanish-speaking cops. Do you speak any Spanish?"

"No, why?"

"I thought you might be able to reassure the woman. She's got to be in a state of terror."

Candy shook her head. "I don't know any Spanish."

I smiled at the Mexican woman. "Okay," I said. "It's okay."

I got out the card that Samuelson had given me and went to the phone. Candy looked panicky. "Can't you keep Sam Felton's name out of it?"

"You're in shock," I said. "Otherwise you'd know better. This is his house. There's a stiff in his living room. Of course I can't keep it out."

"But he's my key witness."

"Not anymore," I said. "Somebody's going to find him dead someplace in a day or so."

"They'll kill him?"

"Absolutely," I said. "That's why Franco took him. You saw how easy it would have been to get him talking. Franco knew that. So do the people that pay Franco. Felton's dead."

"Oh, God," Candy said.

"True," I said. "What we got now is Franco. He'll be harder."

I dialed Samuelson's number. The cop you know is better than the cop you don't know.

Chapter 17

SAMUELSON WAS STILL wearing his tinted glasses even though it was nearly midnight. Besides Samuelson there was a guy from the sheriff's department and two uniformed cops and a lab technician with a camera and a lawyer that KNBS had sent over after Candy called in. One of the uniformed cops with a name tag that said LOPEZ spoke Spanish to the Mexican woman. Samuelson and the sheriff's investigator spoke English to Candy and me. A lot of English.

Samuelson had his coat open and his hands in his hip pockets. The gesture exposed his service revolver, butt forward in its holster on the left side of his belt. He was looking past us through the far windows at the city lights, far below. Bubba had been hauled off by the coroner's people. There was a white chalk outline of his body on the rug. There was a large dark bloodstain inside the outline.

"Let me see if I've got this right now," Samuelson said. He continued to stare past us. "Rafferty saw, or says he saw, Sam Felton make a payoff to a hammer named Franco. He told you. You started investigating. You hired Spenser here—"

The lawyer interrupted. "The station hired Spenser."

Samuelson didn't look at him. "—to keep you out of trouble." He paused, looked sideways at me, said, "Nice job," and went back to staring out the window.

"Despite your warnings," Samuelson continued, "Rafferty pushed Felton and turned up dead. You didn't see any good reason to tell me that, and instead, you and Spenser came over here and questioned Felton until the same hammer, Franco—who had also beaten you up, and who had been following you around, and whom you saw no reason to mention to me—that hammer shows up here with a helper and tried to kidnap you, succeeded in kidnapping Felton while Spenser had the drop on him. And Spenser managed to staple the helper without shooting himself in the elbow. That about fit?"

The lawyer said, "There are several aspects to that summary which imply—"

I said, "Yeah, that's about right."

The lawyer was portly, red-faced, and young, wearing a blue suit of European cut that didn't go with his body and an open-necked white shirt that showed a lot of French cuff.

"Now, listen, I can't represent you if—"

"You represent her," I said. "Not me."

The sheriff's man said, "Aw, for crissake, counselor. Hush up."

The lawyer turned on him. "Now, just one minute, officer. If you think that you can get away with intimidation, you've picked the wrong lawyer."

Samuelson looked at the ceiling.

The sheriff's man said, "Intimidation. That wasn't intimidation. When I intimidate, you'll know it."

The lawyer said, "Are you planning to make a charge against these people, in clear violation of constitutional guarantees?"

"I'll charge them with being a pair of assholes," Samuelson said, "and I'll discuss with the D.A. whether I want to charge them with anything else. How about you, Bernie?"

The sheriff's investigator nodded. "The maid backs

up as much of their story as she knows about. She told Lopez that the big one"—he nodded at me—"shoots very quickly."

"Swell," Samuelson said. "We need another one of those out here."

"Are you looking for Sam Felton?" Candy said.

Samuelson looked at Bernie, the sheriff's man. They both looked at me. "You got any guesses where we might find Felton?" Bernie said.

"Not where," I said. "But I'll bet on his condition."

Samuelson said, "Yeah. Worse than it would have been if you people had talked to me earlier."

"What makes you think they wouldn't have burned him if you people got on his case?"

"'Cause we wouldn't let them," Samuelson said.

"Of course not," I said.

The technician with the camera had packed it away in his tool kit and was leaning on the archway. From the hallway Lopez told Samuelson that he was going to take the maid to her sister's to stay.

Samuelson said, "Well, I'm going home and visit my wife. Don't go anywhere, Spenser. I'll want both of you downtown tomorrow to go through the mug books. I'll talk with the legal guys and we'll see. Miss Sloan is a reporter, and you were protecting her. Lemme say one thing though. To both of you. I don't want even a smell of either one of you anywhere near any aspect of this case forever. You understand?"

"I think you can count on that," the lawyer said.

"I better," Samuelson said. "Because if I can't, I'll bury both of them. That, counselor, is intimidation." He walked out of the room, and the technician and the sheriff's man went with him. All that was left was the lawyer, Candy, me, and the other prowl-car cop who hung around to secure the house.

"Can I give you a lift home, Candy?" the lawyer said.

"No thanks, Keith, I've got my car. I'll take Spenser."

"Okay, fine. Be careful what you say to anyone about this," he said and looked at me.

"Yes, we will, Keith," Candy said. "Good night."

We all went out together and Keith drove off. I got into the MG beside Candy. We drove quietly and slowly back down the winding canyon roads toward Sunset.

"Franco will be in the mug book," I said to Candy. "Guys like him always are."

She was quiet, driving slowly through the dark emptiness of Beverly Hills.

"Once we've got an I.D. on him, the cops will find him. They're good at that."

I wasn't sure she heard me. The top was still down on the MG, and the velvet dark night seemed very low over us.

"Much better than we would be," I said.

There was a rich smell of flowers in the dark air as we went down Beverly Drive. It made me think of funerals. We crossed Wilshire, then Olympic, and pulled in under the entrance portico at the Hillcrest. There was a man to take the car. Duty before sleep. No music filtered down from the rooftop. Candy went into her room and locked the door behind her without a word. I went into mine. It was hot. I turned on the air conditioner and undressed in the dark. When I put my gun on the end table, I could still smell the faint odor of spent ammunition. I didn't like it. Bubba probably hadn't liked it either. If he'd smelled it. Which he probably hadn't.

Chapter 18

WITH A LITTLE computer magic we I.D.'d Franco in about five minutes. They had all the mug shots cross-indexed by names and pseudonyms and in various other ways, and when we fed in the various things we knew, the computer spit out five names. We looked at the five pictures and the third one was Franco. His full name was Francisco Montenegro. His last address was in Hollywood on Franklin Avenue. He was forty-one years old and had been busted six times, two jail terms. All his arrests were for muscle stuff: assault, extortion, twice for murder.

We talked with Samuelson and a detective named Alvarez in Samuelson's office.

"I know Franco," Alvarez said. "He is bad news. He used to be a collector for a loan shark named Leon Ponce, maybe still is. He'll kill people for you, if you'll pay him. Or break bones." He looked at me. "You know the score, don't you? He's like a hundred other guys in this town or yours. Except he's badder than most of them. You're lucky. Most people bang up against Franco, they don't come out ahead."

The phone rang on Samuelson's desk. He answered, listened, said "Okay," and hung up.

"Franco don't live on Franklin anymore," he said. No one seemed surprised. "I called Boston this morning," Samuelson said. "Talked to a homicide sergeant named Belson. He tells me you're legitimate."

"Gee whiz," I said.

"I told him we probably had a case on you for suppressing evidence and asked him what he thought about prosecuting you. He said if it was him, he wouldn't. Said you probably did the world more good outside than inside, but only barely."

"And what did the prosecutor's office say?"

Samuelson grinned. "Said they were too goddamn busy."

"So you're taking Belson's endorsement."

"Yeah."

The phone on Samuelson's desk rang again.

Samuelson said, "Yeah. Yeah. Yeah, that figures. Okay, I'll come out. Yeah." He hung up and said, "They found Felton. In a Dumpster back of a Holiday Inn out in Westwood."

Candy said, "Dead?"

Samuelson nodded. "I'm going out there now," he said. "You're a reporter. Want to come along?"

Candy said, "Let me call the station for a cameraman."

Samuelson indicated his phone. "Dial eight," he said. He looked at me. "That means you'll be along too, huh?"

I nodded.

"If we see a clue anywhere, try not to step on it, okay?"

"I'll just be grateful to watch," I said. "Try to learn a few advanced police techniques."

Candy got off the phone and off we went.

The five levels above the lobby at the Westwood Holiday Inn, on Wilshire, are parking levels, open to the pleasant smell of flowers, with a waist-high wall around each level. You drive down an alley beside the hotel and up a ramp, and there you are. There is no attendant, no limitation on who can drive in. Behind the hotel was a small courtyard with a large Dumpster.

Beyond the Dumpster was a high concrete wall, and beyond that, neat, tile-roofed, mostly stucco houses stretched away down to Santa Monica and beyond. From any of the levels on the back of the hotel, you could see the tower of the Mormon temple building on Santa Monica with the statue of a guy on top of it who was either Joseph Smith or the angel Moroni. It could have been the last thing Sam Felton ever saw.

Felton was where they had found him, spread-eagled, facedown in the Dumpster, dressed as we'd seen him, with some blood dried in the long hair at the back of his head. He was half submerged in trash.

A black detective with a gray-tinged natural and a mustache talked with Samuelson. "I figure he was shot somewhere else, maybe up on one of the parking levels, and dumped in here. If I had to guess, I'd say he got thrown over the edge up there above the Dumpster. He's sunk in pretty good. He must have landed with some impact." The cop looked familiar to me, until I figured out he looked like Billy Eckstine.

"Had a chance to talk with anybody yet?" Samuelson asked.

"Hotel manager says no one reported anything unusual. He wasn't on last night. The night man's on his way in. Haven't talked with the guests yet. Manager sort of doesn't want us to." It couldn't be Billy Eckstine, the voice was all wrong. Maybe if he sang a couple of lines of "I Apologize." I decided not to ask. Nobody was that fond of me here to start with.

"Don't blame him," Samuelson said. "We'll do it anyway. Have the two guys from the black and white start at the top floor. You and your partner start at the bottom. Keep track of the rooms where no one's there. We'll want to see if they've checked out or if they're coming back."

The black detective nodded and went off. A camera-man had showed up to meet Candy. He had a shoulder-mounted camera and a big black shoulder bag and was dressed like he was on his way to a soup kitchen. Except for the on-camera people I'd never seen anyone in television who didn't dress like they got a discount at Woolworth's.

I followed Samuelson up to the first parking level while he began walking around looking at the parapet and the floor and occasionally squatting to look under cars.

"Unless he used an automatic, there won't be any spent shells," I said. "And probably even then he would have picked them up."

Samuelson ignored me.

"You're right, though, that he wouldn't have shot him in the car," I said. "He'd want to avoid getting blood on the upholstery or powder burns or bullet holes. Incriminating."

Samuelson let himself down in a push-up position to look at the cement floor under a white Pontiac Phoenix with a rented-car sticker in the lower left corner of the windshield. He took a long careful look without getting his clothes dirty and stood back up. He brushed his hands off against each other and moved along the parking level. I followed him.

On the third parking level Samuelson found a smear on the low parapet that could have been blood. Below they were getting Felton's body out of the Dumpster. A plainclothes cop in a plaid jacket was watching them alertly. Samuelson yelled down to him.

"Bailey, come up here."

The cop in the plaid jacket sprang into action. When he arrived, Samuelson pointed at the smear. "Find out if it's blood," he said.

Bailey said he'd get right on it. Samuelson kept up his tour. I followed him. Out front, Candy was doing a stand-up in front of the Holiday Inn. The ragamuffin with the camera was about five feet out into Wilshire shooting her, and a cop in uniform was directing traffic around him.

When we got to the top floor of the parking garage and Samuelson was through looking at it, he leaned his forearms on the parapet and stared out at Wilshire Boulevard. Off to the left behind some apartments and a neighborhood of small classy houses you could see UCLA sticking up here and there against the green hills.

"What do you think?" he asked.

"We told you all we knew last night," I said.

"Maybe," he said, "maybe not. But right now I'm interested in opinion. Boston tells me you're a real hot shot. What do you think?"

"I think a lot of what you think. That Franco hauled Felton out of there last night and brought him here and blew him away because Franco was confident Felton would spill everything he knew and some he could make up when folks got to chewing the fat with him, so to speak."

"Yeah?"

"And I think Franco is an employee. He's mean enough, but he's small-time. The thing that Candy's trying to uncover is big-time. Franco's the kind of guy that will shake down whores and unconnected bookies and Mexicans with forged green cards."

Samuelson nodded. "So who employs him?"

"Directly I don't know. Indirectly I would guess the head of Summit Studios."

"Hammond," Samuelson said. "Anything more than you told me last night?"

"No," I said. "He should have known about the offer from Felton either way. He said he didn't. He was too helpful and too innocent and too outraged. He's in it, I'll bet you dinner at Perino's."

"Make it Pink's," Samuelson said. "It's what I can afford if I lose. What about Brewster?"

"I don't know. I only met him once. He could be involved. Any guy who got to where he is can't be too meticulous about things."

"And who's doing the extorting? Who's the money going to?" Samuelson said.

I shook my head. "This is your neighborhood, not mine. Any guesses? How about the guy Franco used to collect for?"

"Leon Ponce? Naw. He's too small-time. Shaking down an outfit like Summit, or Oceania. . . . Leon hasn't got that kind of connections. Or that kind of balls. This is a big-game operation."

Across Wilshire a woman in a pink robe came out onto the balcony of her apartment and watered her plants. She had a transparent plastic bag on her head. Probably just colored her hair.

"Wait a minute," I said.

Samuelson looked at me.

"Shaking down a major movie studio is a big deal, isn't it," I said.

Samuelson nodded. "I just said that."

"But it's not being run like a big-time operation," I said.

"For instance," Samuelson said.

"For instance it's a goddamn mess," I said. "They've beat up a TV reporter and murdered two people including a movie producer. I never heard of Felton, but he can't be totally anonymous."

"Yeah?"

"And sending a lumper like Franco around to collect cash from a producer on location? And being spotted? If the Mob owned Roger Hammond, would they work that way?"

"No," Samuelson said. "Nope, they'd have some stock in the company. They'd have credit transfers and paper transactions I don't even know the names of, and it would take five C.P.A.'s five years to figure out who was getting how much."

"That's right," I said.

"Maybe we been thinking too big," Samuelson said.

"Maybe Franco's starting his own business," I said. "Maybe that's as high as it goes."

"What about that gut feeling about Hammond," Samuelson said. "The dinner you were going to bet at Perino's?"

"I thought it was a chili dog at Pink's," I said.

"That's when I thought I'd lose," Samuelson said.

I shook my head. "Maybe I'm wrong on that. I've been doing this too long to think I don't make mistakes. Hammond is guilty as hell of something. I don't know what. But whether it's got to do with Franco . . ." I shrugged.

"Well," Samuelson said, "we'll start chasing paper. If Felton was paying Franco regularly, the money came from someplace. I'll have someone start on that in the morning. I don't think I've got enough to start digging into Summit's books. All I got is your guess. I'm not sure the courts in California are willing to accept that."

"No wonder," I said, "there's a crisis in our courts."

Chapter 19

CANDY AND I were lunching at the Mandarin in Beverly Hills with a guy named Frederics who was the news director at KNBS. Candy and Frederics both had minced squab. I was working on Mongolian lamb with scallions and drinking Kirin beer. Everything was elegant and cool, including Frederics, who was slicker than the path to hell. His dark hair was parted in the middle and slicked back. He had on a white-on-white shirt with a small round collar and a narrow tie with muted stripes and a white crocheted V-neck sweater tucked into tight Ralph Lauren jeans. The jeans were worn over lizard-skin cowboy boots. I was trying to figure out where he carried his money because no wallet would fit in his pants pocket.

Frederics was drinking white wine with his squab. He took a sip, put the glass down, and said to Candy, "So, after talking with Mark Samuelson and others, the station management—and I agree with them—feels that there's really no further story, and no further danger to you. Mark says you agree with that, Mr. Spenser."

The minced squab was finger food, served in a lettuce leaf, that you picked up and nibbled. Candy nibbled on hers while I answered.

"You're not *the* Frederics of Hollywood, are you?"

Slick as he was, Frederics was, however, not a kidder. He shook his head briefly. "Do you agree with Mark?" he asked.

"Mark, huh?" I looked at Candy. She was still nibbling. "Yeah, I agree with Samuelson that she's probably not in any danger. I'm not sure what I think about there being a story."

"Well, that's a news judgment we'll have to make," Frederics said.

"Yeah."

"So we're taking you off the story, my love," he said to Candy.

"It's still there, John. It's a story that we should be staying on. There's more to it than the police think. Isn't there, Spenser?"

"Of course he'd say so," Frederics said. "His fee is in the balance." He looked at me. "Don't get me wrong. I don't blame you, but you're hardly a disinterested observer."

I asked, "Where do you carry your wallet?"

He said, "Excuse me?"

I said, "Your wallet. Where do you keep it? Your pants are too tight to carry it on your hip."

He said, "Spenser, I invited you to lunch because Candy asked me to. I see no reason to be uncivil."

"Yeah, of course. It's just that you're so damn adorable that I'm jealous. And maybe a little because she busted her ovaries on this thing, and you won't let her clean it up."

"That's a business decision," Frederics said. "And a matter of professional judgment." He looked at Candy. "The judgment has been made and it's final."

I shut up. It was Candy's career, not mine. She looked at the table and didn't speak.

Frederics said to me, "We'll pay you through this week. You've done good work and you deserve a bonus. Expenses, everything. Take a few days and have a good time before you go home."

"I resign," I said.

"What do you mean?"

"I resign. Now. Today. Now. This minute. I don't work for you anymore."

"You don't want the money?"

"Boy, you do have news instincts, don't you," I said.

"You don't want it?"

"That's true," I said.

We were all silent. At the end of the lunch Frederics asked Candy if she had a ride. She said she did. Then Frederics signed the check and we left. I never did see where he carried his wallet. Maybe he didn't. Maybe if you're that slick, you just signed everything. Somebody always had a pen.

Candy said, "You drive."

I said, "You want to go someplace and get drunk?"

She said yes.

I drove east on Wilshire to downtown and found a parking space on Hope Street. The whole way Candy was still silent. The wind ruffled her hair, and she stared straight ahead through the windshield.

I said, "There's a bar on top of the Hyatt-Regency that's nice."

She nodded. We went into the fancy Hyatt lobby and took the elevator up. At a table by the window looking out over downtown L.A., Candy ordered a Jack Daniel's on the rocks. I had a Coors beer. I never cared for Adolph Coors's politics, but I wasn't sure I cared for anyone's, and he made a nice beer. No carcinogens. To the southeast was an old skyscraper done in green stone, like Bullock's on Wilshire, or the Franklin Life Building. Old L.A. Of course old L.A. was maybe 1936. Boston had been around for 306 years by then. On the other hand Rome had been around even longer. Perspective is all.

"What you going to do, babe?" I said to Candy.

"It's there," she said. "The story is there."

"Maybe."

"No maybe. You yourself said Hammond was hiding something."

"Yeah, but maybe what he was hiding isn't what you're looking for."

"I know there's something bad going down at Summit. I know it."

"Woman's intuition?"

She finished the bourbon. "Something," she said. She didn't smile.

"You going to look into it?"

The waitress brought us another round.

Candy drank some more Jack Daniel's. "Maybe you and Samuelson are right about Franco and Felton. Maybe it was just a small-time shakedown. But then why kill him?"

"I don't think killing was a big deal for Franco. Might just have been easier than not killing him."

She shook her head. "No. If he was just doing a simple shakedown, why would Felton have called him? Why would Franco have killed him? He must have wanted something covered up."

I nodded. Nondirective. Me and Carl Rogers.

"All we would have gotten if your theory is true would be evidence of blackmail. Killing Sam Felton would just make matters worse. Franco had to know he'd be the suspect. There's no point being wanted for murder to avoid being wanted for blackmail."

I nodded again. The waitress looked at Candy's empty glass. Candy nodded. She looked at me. I shook my head. The waitress took Candy's empty glass and went for a full one.

"So what he killed Felton for was to cover up something worse than a murder rap," Candy said.

The waitress brought more bourbon. Candy drank some. She turned one hand up and raised her eyebrows at me. "What would be worse than a murder rap?" she said.

"Getting killed," I said.

"Who would kill him?"

"The Mob."

Candy took another sip of bourbon and swished it in her mouth with her cheeks sucked in while she thought about that. Then she swallowed and said, "Why?"

I shook my head. "I don't know. I don't even know that the mob wants to kill him, but think about it this way. A murder rap means being wanted by the cops. If they catch you, they don't usually shoot you. It happens. But not usually. They send you to trial, and it'll take five years to get a conviction if you have any kind of lawyer. And then there's practically no chance of a death penalty. And you might get out in a while for being a nice person. Nobody who's ever been in the joint pretends it's any fun, but it's not the end. If you do something that the Mob doesn't like, that *is* the end. They kill you and sometimes they aren't neat about it."

"So," Candy said. She slurred the *s* a little. "So you're saying that Franco was doing something with Felton that he didn't want the Mob to know about?"

"I'm saying, it's an explanation. Killing Felton to keep the law from finding out something doesn't make sense."

Candy pursed her lips a little bit.

"On the other hand," I said, "guys like Franco often don't make sense. They don't care about hurting people and they sometimes have funny ideas about their reputation or their self-respect. Sometimes they do illogical things."

"Shelf-reshpect?"

"Sure. Lots of real creeps have self-respect. They just have a creepy version of it."

Tears began to form in Candy's eyes. Several of them began to trickle down her face. Her face was starting to crumple up, like a used napkin. She drank some more bourbon.

I said, "You want to get out of here?"

She shook her head.

I said, "Then don't cry. It is very unseemly in a public place to have a crying jag."

She drank the rest of her bourbon. She signaled the waitress and pointed at the empty glass. Then she said to me. "I'm going to the ladies' room and get it together. I won't cry." She had a little trouble pronouncing *ladies*. Then she got up and walked briskly away from the table.

"Another round, sir?" the waitress asked. I nodded. The lounge was nearly empty in midafternoon. It was very cool and still. Few places are more charming than a quiet cocktail lounge in the middle of the day with the ice tinkling in the glasses and the starched look of a bartender's white shirt and the clarity of the beer in the glass with the bubbles drifting up. Soundless below, the noise shut off by glass and distance, the city seemed like something in a stereopticon. Here and there, where the developers had missed, the quintessential look of the twenties and thirties showed through, solid and full of confidence, a little rococo, a little imperial even—between the wars—hopeful even in Depression. Now it was being slowly blotted out by shiny surface, reflecting glass, gloss.

Candy came back from the ladies' room with her makeup fresh and her mouth set in a look of fearsome self-control. She sat and sipped her bourbon. I raised my beer to her.

"Once more unto the breach, dear friend," I said.

She smiled without enthusiasm.

"You want me to stick around," I said.

"I can't pay you."

"It'll count toward my merit badge in covert investigation."

"I really can't."

"It's okay," I said.

"You could move into my apartment," Candy said. "It would save your hotel costs. You already have your ticket home, don't you?"

"Yes."

"I'd pay for the groceries."

"Christ," I said, "I can't afford to leave. It's cheaper than going home."

She sipped some more bourbon. With the glass still near her mouth she looked at me from under her eyebrows and said, "Besides, there could be certain house privileges."

It came out *pribleshes*.

"There goes the merit badge," I said.

Chapter 20

CANDY AND I moved from the Hillcrest to her place on Wetherly Drive. Or I did. Candy was quite sloshed and did little more than stand and sway, first in my room while I packed, then in her room while I packed, then in the elevator while I hauled our luggage down, and in the lobby while I signed the bill. (I felt like John Frederics.)

"We'll send that directly to KNBS, Mr. Spenser," the cashier said.

I nodded as if I were used to that.

In the parking lot I had trouble getting all the luggage into the MG, but I managed with Candy sitting on one of her suitcases, and we drove off to West Hollywood.

Whatever the house privileges were, they weren't forthcoming that evening, because by the time I got the luggage in from the car, she was zonked out on her bed with her clothes still on, lying on her back, snoring faintly. I hung up the stuff from her suitcase that would wrinkle if I didn't. There was nothing to eat in the house, so I went up to Greenblatt's on Sunset and got several roast beef sandwiches and some beer and some bagels and chive cream cheese and blackberry jam for breakfast. I brought it home and ate the sandwiches and drank the beer and read *Play of Double Senses* until eleven and went to sleep on the couch.

I woke up about six in the morning with the weight

of the morning sun on my face. I could hear Candy moving about in the bathroom. I got up and went out to the pool and stripped down to the buff and swam back and forth in the pool for forty-five minutes until I thought I might drown. Then I got out and went in. Candy was back in her bedroom with the door closed. I went in the bathroom, showered off the chlorine, shaved, brushed my teeth, toweled dry, and got dressed.

I was in the kitchen grilling some bagels and percolating some coffee when Candy showed up. She looked as bad as she could, given where God had started her. And I was sure she felt worse than she looked.

"How are you this morning?" I said.

"I threw up," she said.

"Oh."

"What are you making?"

"Bagels," I said, "and chive cream cheese and hot coffee. . . ." Her face had a look of dumb anguish. "You don't want any?" I said. "There's blackberry jam and—"

"You bastard," she said and went out of the kitchen.

I sat at her dining-alcove table and had the toasted bagels with cream cheese and blackberry jam, alternately. Only a barbarian would eat chive cream cheese and blackberry jam on the same bagel.

Candy sat in an armchair in the living room and looked out at her pool with her eyes squinted to slits.

"How about just coffee?" I said.

"No." She held her head quite still. "I need a Coke, or . . . is there any Coke?"

"No."

"Anything? Seven-Up? Tab? Perrier?"

"No. How about a glass of water?"

She shivered, and that seemed to hurt her head. "No," she said, squeezing the word out.

"How about I go up to Schwab's and get you some Alka-Seltzer?"

"Yes."

I finished my bagels and went out and got her the Alka-Seltzer. Then I poured another cup of coffee and sat on her couch with my feet on the coffee table. She drank her Alka-Seltzer. I read the *L.A. Times*. She sat still in the armchair with her eyes closed for maybe an hour, then got up and took two more Alka-Seltzer.

"Two every four hours," I said.

"Shut up." She drank her second glass and went back to her chair.

I finished the coffee and the paper and stood up. She was still quiet in the chair with her eyes closed.

"Now," I said, "about those house privileges."

Without opening her eyes or moving anything but her mouth, she said, "Get away from me."

I grinned. "Okay, do we have any other plans for today?"

"Just give me a little time," she said.

"I'll call Samuelson and see if there's anything developed," I said.

She said, "Mmm."

Samuelson answered his own phone on the first ring. I told him who I was and said, "Do you mind if I call you Mark like John Frederics does?"

Samuelson said, "Who?"

I said, "John Frederics."

He said, "Who's John Frederics?"

I said, "News director? KNBS? Calls you Mark."

"TV newspeople are mostly turkeys," Samuelson said. "I don't know one from another. What do you want?"

I said, "Well, Mark—"

He said, "Don't call me Mark."

"Any sign of Franco Montenegro, Lieutenant?"

"No. And he should be easy, a stiff like him. He's gone. Nobody on the street knows where."

"Would people talk about him?" I asked. "I get the impression he'd be vengeful."

"Vengeful? Christ, you snobby eastern dudes do speak funny. Yeah, he's vengeful, but there's people on the street would tell on Dracula for a couple bucks, or a light sentence, or maybe I look the other way while they're scoring some dope. You know the street, don't you? They got a street in Boston?"

"Boston's where they send," I said, "when the job's too tough for local talent."

"Sure," Samuelson said. "Anyway, us local talent don't have a clue where Franco is."

"You think it's just him, Lieutenant?"

"More and more," he said.

"Then how come he scragged Felton?"

"Yeah," Samuelson said, "that bothers me too, but everything else is right. The more I ask around, the more I look at all the angles, the more it looks like a small-time shakedown that went sour."

"You got a theory on why he scragged Felton?"

"No. Maybe I never will have. I'm a simple copper, you know. I don't think everything always fits. I take the best answer I can get. Guys like Franco do funny things. They aren't logical people."

"Yeah," I said. "But it still bothers me."

"Bothers me too," Samuelson said, "but I do what I can. You hear anything, let me know. And try and keep the goddamn broad out of the way, will you?"

"She's been taken off assignment," I said. "This afternoon we're going out to cover a pet show at the Santa Monica Auditorium."

"Good," Samuelson said. "Try not to get bit." He hung up.

I looked at Candy. "Nothing on Franco," I said. "Samuelson doesn't like him killing Felton either."

The phone rang and I picked it up. "Sloan House," I said.

The voice of an elegant woman said, "Miss Sloan, please. Mr. Peter Brewster calling."

I said, in my Allan Pinkerton voice, "One moment, please."

I put my hand over the mouthpiece and said to Candy, "Peter Brewster?"

She stared at me a minute as if I'd wakened her. Then she said softly, "God," and then got up and walked over firmly and took the phone.

"Yes? . . . Yes. . . . Hello, Mr. Brewster. . . . It's okay, Mr. Brewster. . . ." The color began to come back into Candy's face as she talked. "No, it's okay. I understand. Lots of people have that reaction. . . . Yes. I told him that." She looked sideways at me for a moment. "Why, certainly . . . I'd love it. Sure. Four North Wetherly Drive. I'll be ready. . . . Thank you. . . . Yes. You too. Bye."

She hung up. I was standing with my arms folded, looking at her.

She said, "Peter Brewster wants to take me to dinner."

I raised my eyebrows.

She said, "He's sorry he overreacted the other day and wants a chance to behave better."

"Where are you dining?" I said.

"I don't know. He'll pick me up here at seven."

"Okay, leave me your keys and I'll tail you."

She widened her eyes at me. "You think it could be dangerous?"

"Even if it isn't, it'll be good practice for me," I said.

Candy nodded absently. "Okay," she said. "What shall I wear?"

"A gun," I said.

— 131 —

Chapter 21

BREWSTER SHOWED UP at 7:02 in a black Cadillac sedan with a driver. Democrat that he was, Brewster came to the door personally. I was already in the MG when he arrived, around the corner on Phyllis Street with the motor idling. I couldn't see any reason for Brewster to harm Candy, but I hadn't seen any reason why Franco would want to harm Felton either. So I'm not Philo Vance, so what?

He took her to Perino's. I owed myself a beer. I'd bet either Perino's or Scandia. The driver let them out and drove away. I parked on Wilshire heading downtown and watched the front door of the restaurant in my rearview mirror.

There was little traffic on Wilshire. There was no one walking. The stars came out and the moon gleamed at me. I idled the motor and listened to a Dodger game and thought about things. Brewster could be taking Candy out to dinner because she was good-looking and sexy, and he wanted to get her into bed with him. Or he could be taking her out to dinner to see if he could find out how much she really knew about his affairs so that he could decide if she was a danger to him. Brewster was a good-looking guy, and he had money and power, and he was probably used to getting along well with women, which got me nowhere because it covered either possibility. Brewster probably wouldn't do Candy any damage himself. If he decided she was dangerous, and he wanted something done, he'd have it done. He was, after all, an executive. Still, there was no harm sticking close. Better safe than sorry, my mother used to tell me. Although I think she was talking about girls.

At nine forty-five the Cadillac rolled up in front of Perino's. Small airplanes could land on its hood; in case of war all of Liechtenstein could escape in it. The maître d' opened the front door and acted solicitous, and Candy came out ahead of Brewster. She had chosen a bright green tuxedo-looking suit and a beaded something-or-other with no straps for a blouse and very high-heeled silver shoes. The light from the open restaurant door made her blond hair gleam.

She carried a small silver purse and in it, I knew, was the Colt .32 I had taken from the late Bubba. We'd had a brief weapons drill about five o'clock, just before she started getting ready to go out. She hadn't been too keen on it. It was heavy and made a lump in her purse. "Why will I need it at Perino's?" she had said.

"The soup may be cold," I had said. And we had argued until she was in such a rush to start getting ready that she had given in.

She was laughing when she came out, her head thrown back a little toward Brewster behind her. Apparently she hadn't had to use the gun yet. She was holding his hand. The driver got out and held the door of the Caddy open for them, and they got in. The driver went around and got in and drove west on Wilshire. I U-turned and followed them. At ten o'clock on a Wednesday evening Wilshire Boulevard was so empty of traffic, you could have U-turned a nuclear submarine without a problem. That made trailing them a little harder because there wasn't much traffic to hide in. I dropped a long way back until a third car pulled in between us from a side street, and then I closed behind the third car.

Brewster lived on Roxbury Drive between Lomitas and Sunset in a big stucco and frame house with an arched portico on one side over the driveway. The Caddy went up through the portico, and I drove on past. I parked at the corner of Sunset and watched in the mirror. The Caddy didn't reappear. I cruised back down Roxbury Drive and looked in under the portico. There was no sign of the Caddy. Must be around back. Probably had its own hangar.

I drove on down to Lomitas and parked around the corner and looked back at Brewster's house.

I had a problem. Maybe several. This wasn't the kind of neighborhood where a strange car can park for hours without a cop stopping by and looking in on you. And God only knew what would happen if the Bel-Air Patrol caught me. I could try to slip in and get a look at what was happening in Brewster's house, but in this kind of neighborhood, and Brewster being that kind of guy, the place would be burglar-alarmed and electronically protected. Probably dragons in the moat.

I went around the block again. Three doors down from Brewster was a house with a flat-white front that looked like a pumping station for the Guadalajara Water District. It had several days worth of newspapers scattered on the front lawn. I pulled into the driveway and parked. There was no activity in the house. The newspapers were a giveaway. If there was somebody in the house, it was probably a burglar. I got out of the car and walked back toward Brewster's. There were no lights showing in front. I walked briskly up the driveway, under the portico, and around back. The Caddy was parked on a brick turnaround near a garage that was built to look like a stable. It was empty. There was a second story to the garage, and in one of the windows a light shone. Chauffeur's quarters. The yard rolled away to my left. No wider than a football field, but at least as long. Down toward the other end zone was a swimming pool and some tennis courts and a cabana beyond them. Closer to me in the bright moonlight was a croquet lawn. At the far end of the house, on my right, a light shone in a corner room. I walked down toward it, trying to look like I was supposed to be there. I needed a clipboard. If you have a clipboard and three pens in your shirt pocket you can go anywhere and do anything and no one will bother you.

There were some flowery shrubs around that corner of the house. I slipped inside them and looked in the window. Candy and Brewster were on the couch. On a coffee table in front of them was a bottle of Courvoisier, a siphon of seltzer, a bowl of ice, and two glasses. Candy and Brewster weren't drinking. They were necking. On the couch. I blushed. The necking got heavier. Inelegant. Not classy, like dancing on a hotel balcony. I looked away and leaned against the house. Now what? Candy didn't seem to be in real danger unless Brewster was planning to feel her to death. But what about later? I looked back in the window. Candy was partially undressed. I felt like the photo editor at *Hustler*. I looked up at the moon. *On the couch?* I thought. *Jesus Christ! The sophisticated superrich.* I looked once more. They were naked. Making love. On the couch.

I had a full file of Dick Tracy crime-stoppers at home, but none of them that I could remember covered this. What would Allan Pinkerton do? What would I tell the Bel-Air Patrol if they put the arm on me here in the bushes? My palms felt a little sweaty. I squinted a little to blur things and took a quick peek. They were still at it. Private eye was one thing, Peeping Tom was another. I headed for the car.

I was still sitting in it in the driveway of the empty house at twenty minutes of four when the Caddy pulled out of the driveway and turned right. It turned right again at Sunset, and I could see it heading east on Sunset when I turned the corner as far behind it as I could get without losing sight. I couldn't see who was in it, and it could have been a fake to lead me away, but the best guess was that it was taking Candy home. It was also the right guess.

I waited up on Sunset while the chauffeur opened the door and escorted Candy in. He came back out, got in the Caddy, went on down Wetherly, and disappeared around the corner on Phyllis. Then I pulled up in front of Candy's house and parked.

Candy let me in on the first knock. "Were you behind me all the way?" she said.

"All the way," I said. She looked about as she had when she left nine hours ago. Her lipstick was fresh. Her clothes were neat. Her hair was smooth. She smelled wonderfully of perfume and good brandy, and her eyes sparkled.

"I didn't dare look for you. I saw you outside Perino's but that's all. It's a funny feeling being shadowed."

"That's me," I said. "The shadow. The weed of crime bears bitter fruit."

"He's a really charming man," Candy said.

I nodded.

"He's very sure, if you know what I mean. Very in-charge. He seems to have been everywhere. He seems to know everyone."

"Who knows," I said, "what evil lurks in the hearts of men."

"I can't even remember that program. I've just heard nostalgia records."

I said, "So you like old Peter, do you?"

"No," she said. "I don't like him at all. But he likes me and he thinks I like him, and I'm going to let him

— 136 —

keep thinking so until I can nail him right to the floor." As she spoke her face looked very flat and tight, and the cheekbones seemed more prominent.

I found a beer in the refrigerator and draped myself in Candy's armchair and let one foot hang over the arm and drank some beer.

"Did you get a sense of what he was after?" Nice phrasing.

Candy nodded. "I think he's trying to find out what I know."

"He any good at it?"

"Not bad," Candy said, "but I've been hustled by people who were better. Although most of them were just after my body."

I nodded.

"I'm sorry you had to sit around outside until four in the morning," Candy said.

I shrugged.

"Aren't you going to ask me what I did in there until four in the morning?"

"I know already," I said.

She raised her eyebrows at me.

"I peeked in the window," I said.

Candy turned red. "You watched?"

"Briefly," I said.

She was very flushed now, "Did you see us . . . ?"

"Yeah," I said. "For a minute."

She was silent for a moment. "Well," she said, "you didn't see anything you hadn't already seen, did you?"

"The angle was different," I said.

Her face got hard again, the way it had when she spoke of nailing Brewster. "Turn you on?" she said.

I shook my head. "No. Embarrassed me. I didn't want to lose sight of you and I didn't want to watch. I settled for sitting in the car."

Her face was still hard. "Disapprove?"

"I don't know. I might," I said. "I don't disapprove of you screwing somebody. I might disapprove of you screwing somebody in order to nail him to the floor."

"You make me laugh," she said. "All of you."

"All of me?" I drank the rest of the beer.

"Men," she said. "It's not women who are silly about sex. It's men. You think it ought to be important." She stretched the word into three spaced and portentous syllables. "Women don't. Women know it's useful."

I went to the kitchen for another beer. "Sounds sexist to me," I said from the refrigerator.

"Why? If I use what I've got to exploit men and further my interests, why is that sexist? They have strength, we have sex. They don't hesitate to use strength."

I sat back in the chair. "Okay," I said. "Want a sip of my beer?"

She shook her head. "You haven't got an argument, have you? So you just change the subject."

"I'm a romantic," I said. "Arguments are useless with romantics. You want a sip?"

"No," she said. She stood staring at me. I drank my beer. "You still disapprove, don't you?"

"I do the best I can to approve and disapprove only of my own behavior. I don't always succeed, but I try. I'm trying now and I'm going to keep at it. How about a whole can for yourself?"

"I don't like beer," she said.

Chapter 22

CANDY HAD TO be at work at noon. I went with her. Since she was convinced that Brewster was trying to find out what she knew, there was reason to suppose she might still need protection. Especially if he figured out that, while he was trying to find out what she knew, she was trying to find out what he knew.

We spent the first hour of the afternoon walking along Broadway, Candy walking with the wife of a Mexican-American congressional candidate, talking or pretending to while the cameras cranked. Candy asked several questions while the cameras zoomed in. I was lurking around, out of camera range, alert in case a captain of industry lunged from the crowd and hurled Candy on a couch. The candidate's wife didn't bother to answer the questions. She'd done this before and she knew the real interview would take place someplace else and would then be dubbed over the pictures of them walking. Then we all drove back to KNBS studios, where Candy taped the interview and they shot some reverses, and then a car took the candidate's wife home.

At eight o'clock Brewster and his driver and his Caddy came by the studio and took her to a Dodger game, where they sat in his private box. Or I assumed they sat in his private box. He was the type. But I had no way to know, because I never got into the game. I sat in the MG in the parking lot listening on the radio, and at about eleven followed them back to his place and then went back to Candy's and let myself in with her key and went to sleep. We had agreed before we started out that morning that there was no point in me hanging around in the bushes at Brewster's house. If he was going to do her damage, I'd be no use to her there anyway. At least here she could phone me.

She didn't come home that night at all. I felt like somebody's worried father until she came home at seven fifteen in the morning amid the chirping birds.

That day I hung around while Candy interviewed a rape victim, talked to the chairwoman of an educational-reform group, did a stand-up in front of a new boutique that had opened in Beverly Hills, and interviewed a glossy-looking kid who had just finished shooting the pilot for a TV series that was coincidentally going to be carried locally on KNBS-TV. Then I hung around the studio while Candy did some film editing and taped some narration over some of the edited film, and spent maybe a half hour in conference with Frederics, the news director.

That evening I finished up my book on Edmund Spenser while Brewster took Candy to the revival of a Broadway musical at the Music Center.

The next day Candy covered a blood shortage at the L.A. Red Cross blood bank, a Right to Life protest outside an abortion clinic in El Monte, a benefit fashion show staged by the wives of the California Angels, and the finals of a baton-twirling contest in Pasadena.

That evening she went with Brewster to a party at Marina del Rey. I stopped at a drugstore on La Brea near Melrose and bought a copy of *The Great Gatsby* off the paperback rack. I hadn't read it in about five years, and it was time again. I picked up some tomatoes, lettuce, bacon, and bread at Ralph's, along with a six-pack of Coors and a jar of mayonnaise, and went back to Candy's apartment to an orgy of B.L.T.'s. And elegant prose. And beer.

Candy called from the station the next morning around nine to tell me that she'd be at the station most of the day, and there was no need for me to hang around there. Station security was enough protection.

"I'll be home this evening, though," she said. "Brewster's out of town until Thursday."

I told her I'd pick her up when it was time. And she said she'd call. And I hung up. I had finished *Gatsby* in a sitting. With breakfast I'd read the *L.A. Times*. I was irritated, bored, restless, edgy, useless, frustrated, bewitched, bothered, and bewildered. I wasn't making any money. I wasn't solving a crime. I wasn't saving a widow or an orphan. I was sleeping on a couch and my back was getting stiff. I thought about packing it in and going home. I could be having dinner with Susan this evening. I looked at my suitcase, tucked in between the couch and the wall. Ten minutes to pack, ten minutes to get a cab, half hour to the airport. I could make the noon flight easy. I shook my head. Not yet. There was something besides coitus happening in the Sloan-Brewster romance, and I had to stay around until I found out what.

But in the meantime I had to get rid of the feeling that my gears were grinding to a halt. I put on my running stuff and did about ten minutes of stretching and then went up to Sunset and headed west at an easy pace. You run out of sidewalk on Sunset, and the traffic is too ugly to run in the street, so I shifted down a block to Lomitas and went along amid the affluence to Whittier Drive, down Whittier to the place where it joins Wilshire by the Beverly Hilton Hotel. I went along Wilshire to Beverly Glen, up Beverly Glen, and started cruising among the neighborhoods of Westwood until I ended up on Le Conte Avenue in front of UCLA Medical Center. The sun was hot, and the sweat had soaked pleasingly through my T-shirt. The hills in Westwood were just right. You'd barely notice them in a car, but it was a good varied workout running. I took it easy, ten twelve-minute miles, sightseeing. I U-turned at Westwood Boulevard and jogged back east along Le Conte. There were orange trees, ripe with fruit in people's front yards, and lemon trees, and now and then an olive tree with small black fruit on it. The roofs of the houses were mostly red tile, the siding often white stucco, the yards immaculate. There was no residue of sand and salt from the winter's snow. The driveways often slanted up, without fear of ice. "He sent us this eternal spring,/Which here enamels everything." Who had written that? Not Peter Brewster. I jogged along just fast enough to pass someone walking. Except, like everywhere else in Tinsel Town, no one was walking. Somewhere I heard two dogs barking. Probably a recording. "He hangs in shades the orange bright,/Like golden lamps in a green light." The houses were close together. I never figured out why. There was space abounding out here at the fag end of the way west. Why did everyone huddle together? Why didn't they ever come out on the street? How could they produce something as silly as Rodeo Drive? Would Candy elope with Peter Brewster?

It was early afternoon when I got back to Candy's. I'd done about fifteen miles and I felt better. I spent a long time in Candy's shower. Then I got dressed and took Candy's car and went out for a drive. I had read that morning in the *L.A. Times* that traffic congestion was a leading tourist complaint in L.A. They were obviously not tourists from the East. Compared to Boston and New York, driving in L.A. was like driving in Biddeford, Maine. The freeways were bad, but I never had occasion to use them. I drove east on Hollywood Boulevard, slowly, past Vermont Avenue, where

Hollywood fuses with Sunset, and on along Sunset toward downtown L.A. I got off by the Dorothy Chandler Pavilion and drove around downtown a little and then headed back on Third Street. I'd been a lot of places and there were usually resemblances. Boston and San Francisco had points of comparison, and they were both not unlike New York, only smaller, and New York was not unlike London, only newer. But L.A. was like nothing I'd ever seen. I didn't know any place like it for sprawl, for the apparently idiosyncratic mix of homes and businesses and shopping malls. There was no center, no fixed point for taking bearings. It ambled and sprawled and disarrayed all over the peculiar landscape—garish and fascinating and imprecise and silly, smelling richly of bougainvillea and engine emissions, full of trees and grass and flowers and neon and pretense. And off to the northeast, beyond the Hollywood Hills, above the smog, and far from Disneyland were the mountains with snow on their peaks. I wondered if there was a leopard frozen up there anywhere.

The top was down and the wind was warm on my face. I turned down La Brea and parked and walked along Wilshire to the La Brea Tar Pits with their huge plastic statues half sunk in the tar. There was a museum there, and I went in and looked at the relics and the dioramas and the graphics until about four. Then I went back outside. A young man wearing Frye boots and a cowboy hat who had never seen a cow was playing banjo loudly and not well. He had the banjo case open on the ground near him for contributions. It wasn't very full. In fact what was in there was probably what he'd seeded it with. Some kids hung around while he played "Camptown Races" and then drifted off. The banjo player didn't seem to mind.

I got back in the MG and drove back to Candy's apartment feeling friendly toward L.A. It was a big sunny buffoon of a city; corny and ornate and disorganized but kind of fun. The last hallucination, the dwindled fragment of—what had Fitzgerald called it? —"the last and greatest of all human dreams." It was where we'd run out of room, where the dream had run up against the ocean, and human voices woke us. Los Angeles was the butt end, where we'd spat it out with our mouths tasting of ashes, but a genial failure of a place for all of that.

I had drunk two beers in Candy's living room when she called and asked me to pick her up.

"Dress up," she said. "I'm going to take you to dinner."

"Tie?" I asked.

"It's permitted," she said.

Chapter 23

WE HAD DINNER at Ma Maison, which looks like the cook tent for a Rotary barbecue and is so *in* that it has an unlisted phone. There were several famous people there and many young good-looking women with older out-of-shape men. The food was admirable.

"You don't see Rudd Weatherwax in the restaurant, do you?" I said to Candy.

"I never heard of him," she said.

"*Sic transit gloria*," I said. "Is that . . . ?"

Candy nodded. "Somewhat more of her these days."

"She shouldn't swim during whaling season," I said.

Candy smiled. We finished our asparagus vinaigrette. The waiter brought us veal medallions and poured some more of the white Bordeaux we'd ordered.

"Good," Candy said. "What kind is it?"

"Graves," I said.

"I've got the goods on Peter," Candy said.

There were pan-fried potatoes with the veal that were the best I'd ever had. I ate one. "The goods?"

Her face was bright. "Yes. I've got him, I think. But I need you to help."

"Glad to," I said. "It'll ice my merit badge. What have you got him for?"

"One reason I've tried to be with him every night is I wanted to get him won over before you got bored and went home. I knew I'd need you and I had to hurry."

"Bored? Me? I haven't even been to Knott's Berry Farm yet."

"Well, last night it paid off. He got drunk and started talking about how powerful and important he was. He's gotten blackout drunk every time I've been with him. I think he might have thought he was being sly, and seeing if I would talk about my interest in him. But he kept drinking and he got carried away. Every time it's the same. We make love. Then he drinks and struts around and conducts a monologue on how important he is. Talked about his connections, with politicians, with mobsters, movie stars. How he could get anything fixed or have someone killed if he wanted to. He bragged about some of the actresses he'd slept with."

"Mala Powers?" I said.

"No."

"Phew."

"But I was in good company," she said.

"Did he get specific about other things?" I asked.

"Yes. He said, for instance, that he knew where Franco was. He used his full name."

"Montenegro," I said.

"Yes. He said he knew how to get Franco Montenegro. He said Franco had made a mistake, and he was going to regret it."

"And?"

"And, well, it's boring to do it word for word, but I found out that Franco called him and demanded money or he'd tell the police about Peter's Mob connections. Brewster's going to meet him tomorrow."

"And Brewster's going to go himself?"

"Franco insisted."

"Where is he going to meet him?"

"I don't know," Candy said. "But I'm having dinner

with Peter tomorrow, and if I can find out when he's going to meet Franco, I thought we could follow him."

"If Franco spots us behind Brewster, he'll think he's been sold out and might air old Peter right on the spot."

"It's a chance I'll take," Candy said.

"As long as you can nail Brewster to the floor," I said.

Candy put her fork down and looked at me. "Don't use that tone with me," she said. "Peter Brewster is a completely corrupt man, and I'm going to catch him. If there's risk to him in that, so be it. Life's sometimes risky."

"What exactly are we going to catch him at?"

"I don't know the legal mumbo jumbo. Consorting with a known criminal. Abetting an escaped felon. Conspiracy. You should know better than I do."

"Brewster won't go alone to see Franco," I said.

"Franco said he had to, or he'd go straight to the cops."

I shook my head. "Franco won't go to the cops and Brewster knows it. Brewster will bring somebody, probably Simms, and if he's as bad as you say he is, he'll try to put Franco away."

"Why doesn't Franco go to the police?"

"Because he's desperate. Because he needs money bad enough to risk blackmailing Brewster, and he's not going to throw it away. If Franco goes to the cops, he's lost his blackmail. And Brewster will kill him if he can—or if he and his helpers can—because as long as Franco is out there, he's like a loaded gun pointing at Brewster."

The waiter brought us a pear tart and coffee.

"Franco needs money to get out of town," Candy said. It was a half question.

"I'd guess," I said. "Or maybe just to live. When you're hiding, it's hard to earn a salary."

"But if Simms helps him kill Franco, then won't Simms know that Brewster's"—she spread her hands—"a criminal?"

"Sure, but he probably knows it now. If Brewster's Mob-connected, then I'd guess Simms is probably a Mob watchdog anyway."

"You mean the Mob owns Peter?"

"It's rarely the other way around," I said.

Candy paid the checks and we left Ma Maison. A kid brought Candy's car around and we got in. Candy drove. We went out Melrose, across Santa Monica to Doheny, and up Doheny to Candy's place. Neither one of us said anything as we drove.

In her apartment Candy said, "Shall we have a little brandy and soda?"

I said, "Sure."

She made two drinks. We took them out and sat by the pool and drank.

"You've been on the couch for some time now," Candy said.

"Yes."

"Is it uncomfortable?"

"Sort of," I said.

"I'm sorry," Candy said.

The pool filter made a small slurping sound as water trickled into the skimmer.

"Not your fault," I said. "Furniture makers have no pride of craftmanship anymore."

"I mean that I've been away with Peter, not with you."

"A job's a job," I said.

"Would you care to move into the bedroom tonight?" she said.

I shook my head. "No," I said. "Thanks, but I'll stick with the couch."

Her face went tight again, with lines around her mouth. "Why?"

"It's something I'd be ashamed to tell Susan."

"You weren't ashamed last time. Is it Peter Brewster?"

"Partly."

"It's not Susan, is it? You're just jealous."

"I don't think so," I said. "See, once, on a warm night in a strange city with music drifting down—that's fun. Or it was for me. But a live-in arrangement—'house privileges,' I think you called it—when you apologize for being"—I made a word-groping gesture with my hands—"inattentive—that's unfaithfulness."

"I think it's nothing that noble," Candy said. "You're no different that all the others. You're jealous. You can't stand sharing me with Peter."

"If that were true," I said, "what better reason to sleep on the couch. If we've gone to a point where I'm jealous of you, then I am cheating. I don't want to be jealous of anyone but Suze. I shouldn't be."

Candy shook her head. "That's crap," she said. "You insist on making everything sound fancy. Always guff about honor and being faithful and not being ashamed. Everything you do becomes some kind of goddamn quest for the Holy Grail. It's just self-dramatization. Self-dramatization so you don't have to face up to how shabby your life is, and pointless."

"Well, there's that," I said.

"And goddamit, don't patronize me. When I score a point, you ought to be man enough to admit it."

"Person enough," I said. "Don't be sexist."

"So you've decided just to joke about it. You know you can't win the argument, so you make fun."

"Candy, I am a long way past the point where I see the world in terms of debating points. I don't care if I win or lose arguments. Sleeping with you again would be cheating on Susan, at least by my definition,

— 149 —

and by hers. That's sufficient. You're just as desirable as you ever were. And I'm just as randy. But I am stern of will. So lemme sleep on the couch and stop being offended."

"You self-sufficient bastard," she said.

"Yes," I said.

"But you'll help me tomorrow?"

"Yes," I said.

Chapter 24

I WENT WITH Candy to the studio in the morning. She drove. I looked around.

"I am going to stay as close as I can," I said. "Even if I'm spotted, it's better than you getting burned."

"You really think there's that kind of danger?"

"You betcha," I said. "Brewster may remember what he told you and if he does, you're a real threat to him."

"But he thinks I'm in love with him."

"After five days?" I said.

"He thinks everyone is in love with him anyway. He assumes conquest."

"I'll accept that," I said. "And I'm willing to concede that Brewster's not very smart. Tycoons often aren't, I've found. But they are also rarely sentimental. Even if he thinks you are permanently smitten with his wonderful self, what's he lose by having you shot?"

"Thanks a lot."

"It's not denigrating you. It's denigrating him. He doesn't cherish you. He doesn't cherish anything. He can replace you with some worshipful starlet later this evening if he needs to. He wouldn't differentiate."

Candy was quiet.

"Think about it. What does he want from you?"

"Sex."

"Yeah, and what else?"

"Admiration. He wants me to tell him how masterful he is. He wants me to go *ooh* at how much money and clout he has."

"And if he didn't have you to do that, what?"

"He'd get someone else."

"Is it your brains and wit and perception and strength he needs?"

"No."

We pulled into the parking lot behind the station. "So what is it you give him?"

"I look good in public," Candy said. "I do good in bed. And I hang on his every word."

"How many other women in Hollywood could fill that role?"

"A trillion," Candy said.

"So be careful," I said. "And don't get into places I can't follow."

Candy nodded and we went into the studio.

There was a staff meeting scheduled for much of the morning, and I left Candy to deal with that. It was probably as deadly in its way as Brewster, but it wasn't the kind of deadliness I could ameliorate.

I took a cab from the station to a Hertz agency and rented a Ford Fairlane that looked like every third car on the road. The MG was too conspicuous now. It had been following Brewster too long. Driving back to KNBS, I stopped at a Taco Burro stand and had a bean and cheese burrito for lunch. With coffee. Authenticity is not always possible.

During the afternoon I drove down to Marineland with Candy. We met a camerawoman there, and Candy did a piece on a killer whale that had been born there during the week.

"Glamor," I said to Candy on the long ride back. "You show-biz folks lead lives of such glamor and sophistication."

She was driving. She said, "Do you really think Peter Brewster might try to kill me?"

"Yes."

We were going north on the Harbor Freeway. The road was made of large asphalt squares, and the wheels as they hit the intervaled seams made a kind of rhythmic thump.

"I'm scared," she said.

"Then why continue? Why not go to Samuelson with what you've got and let him take the weight for a while?"

"What have I got exactly?" Candy said.

"You know he's Mob-connected," I said. "You may have stumbled in by accident. Franco and Felton may have had nothing to do with it. But you're in. He's spilled that he's on the dirty side, and if he remembers that, you're already a danger to him."

The tires made their thump. With the top down the hot wind was a steady push on my face.

"I can't," Candy said. "I've invested too much. It means too much."

"You'd still break the story," I said. " 'Acting on a tip from newsperson Candy Sloan, police today . . .' It would read good," I said.

She was quiet. She passed a sign that said TORRANCE. Traffic was heavy going the other way, coming out of L.A., going home for a beer and maybe water the lawn. Barbecue some ribs maybe. See what was on the tube later. Might be a ball game. Get the kids to bed. Turn up the air conditioning. Settle in and watch the Angels. Maybe another beer. Maybe before bed a sandwich, maybe a hug from the wife.

"I can't," Candy said. "I can't do it that way. It would be too girlie-girl. Would you turn it over to the police?"

"Not yet," I said.

"So you understand, perhaps, why I won't."

"Understand, yes. Approve, no."

"Even though you'd be the same way?"

"Just because I'm peculiar doesn't mean you should be. This is what cops draw their pay for. The smart way is to let them earn it."

"Stand on the sidelines and look pretty while the men play ball?"

"Sex is not at issue here," I said. "Danger is."

"If I don't follow this through, I add credence to what practically everyone thinks. You don't know what it's like in television. It's a male domain. All the decision-makers are male. And every goddamn one of them assumes I'm good for interviewing baby whales. Every goddamn one of them that I've ever met assumes, when the going gets rough, I'll tuck my skirts up and run."

"And you're going to prove them wrong."

"Absolutely," she said.

"Okay," I said.

We left the Harbor Freeway and headed north on the San Diego Freeway. It was nearly seven when we got to Candy's place. She parked and set the brake and looked at me.

"You'll stick, won't you?" she said.

"Yes."

"Even though I'm not paying you?"

"Yes."

"I could pay you a little bit each month for a year or so, maybe."

"I could give you one of those little payment books like the banks do," I said. "No money down, thirty-six easy payments. Budget Rent-a-Sleuth."

"I'm serious."

"I don't need the money," I said. "The station paid me fine."

We were still sitting in the car in front of her house. She was looking at me. "And you'll stay until it's finished?" she said.

"Yes."

"For no pay."

"Yes."

"And I'm not sleeping with you?"

"Despite that," I said.

"Why?"

"I like you. You need help. It's help I can supply."

She looked at her watch. "My God," she said. "It's seven o'clock. Peter will be here in fifteen minutes." She was out of the car and heading for the house in that peculiar female run that high heels produce.

I went and sat in my rented Fairlane down the street on the other side and waited. I was thinking wistfully of the burrito I'd had for lunch, when Brewster arrived. He wasn't in the Caddy. He was driving himself in a dark green Mercedes 450 SL.

No one was with him. *Why not?* Why had he changed his pattern? Was he going to do something that he did not want witnessed? I was not pleased. Brewster didn't seem to mind. He went up to the door at a brisk pace as if he didn't care whether I was ever pleased by anything. In five minutes he came out with Candy on his arm. They got in the Mercedes and drove off.

Chapter 25

OFF SEPULVEDA BOULEVARD, out toward the airport, visible from the street, there are some vestigial oil rigs —still pumping—reminders that all the money in L.A. didn't come from movies.

I tailed Brewster and Candy out there and onto a side road. The side road forked one hundred yards in from Sepulveda. Brewster took the left fork. Far down the road I saw his taillights stop and then darken. I took the right fork, went around a bend, parked, and headed back on foot.

The oil pumps were all around now in the dim evening, making very little sound, unattended, rocking without apparent cause, slightly saurian. I went in among them, cutting across the small field toward the other fork where Brewster had parked. I could feel the tension skitter along my backbone and bunch in the muscles around my shoulders. This was no place to bring a date. Brewster was too old to go parking. I hadn't seen a picnic basket.

I moved carefully in the dark, trying to make no sound. I was in business clothes—a dark blue sweat shirt with the sleeves cut off, blue jeans, and dark blue jogging shoes. No bright colors. I'd left my Windbreaker in the car. I didn't care if people saw my gun. In fact I rather hoped they would, and be impressed.

The sounds of planes coming and going from LAX made a near, steady noise above us. So steady, it faded into background, and you only noticed it when it paused. I saw Brewster's car. The lights were out. The doors were closed. I moved up very carefully behind it and looked in the window. It was empty. I stood stock-still and listened. The sound of airplanes. The sound of the wells pumping. The sound, faintly, of traffic on the San Diego Freeway beyond Sepulveda. No other sound.

I crouched behind the car and tried to see in among the pumps. The stars were out, but there was no moon, and there wasn't much light. There were no streetlights on this road, and no houses anywhere in sight. The steadily moving apparatus of the wells was alien and hostile in the darkness.

I moved in among the oil rigs, placing each foot very carefully as I went. I listened after every step, but all I heard was an increasing wind. It made odd noises among the oil pumps as it came, hot and steady and affectionless, a bit eerie as it moved through the anachronistic machinery. The ground in the oil field was soft dirt, and as the wind stiffened, it picked up dust and moved it around. I began to move faster and less carefully. I was getting scared. Candy had been in there alone with Brewster too long. The wind was coming harder now, as if reinforcements had caught up with the advance breeze. It rattled loose cabling on the oil rigs. I began to run, dodging equipment as I did, trying to cut diagonally across the oil field so that I'd cover as much in one sweep as I could. Except I didn't know the size or shape of the field and therefore didn't know what a diagonal was. I was squinting against the blowing dirt. I had my gun in my hand. And I was trying to fight down the sense of urgency that was pushing up my throat. Clouds that must have ridden in with the wind began to gather over the stars, and the oil yard became even darker. I had to slow down. I could barely see the length of my foot-fall in front of me and I wouldn't help Candy much if I ran head-on into one of the pumps. In places the footing was mucky and slippery, and there was a fetid smell that the wind was not able to drive away.

As I moved in the darkness I noticed that there was scrub growth in parts of the oil field. When I was very close, I could see them and see how the wind made their shapes contort as their branches moved restively, like animals too long restrained. Then I heard the shots. The sound sat on top of the wind the way a bird sits on a power line. I whirled, looking for muzzle flash, and spotted some over to my left as more shots rode in on the wind. I ran toward them, my gun out. Two more shots. I banged into the superstructure of one of the pumps and spun around and staggered and kept my feet and kept going toward the spot where the memory of muzzle flash still vibrated in my mind. There was a brief flare of what must have been head-lights swinging away, and then only the wind sound and the darkness. The wind had cooled, and there was thunder rolling to the west, and a new smell of rain in the air. I stopped for a moment and listened, staring toward the place where I'd seen the muzzle flashes and the headlights. Then lightning made a jagged flash, and I saw a car parked ahead of me. I moved toward it. I reached the car before the thunder caught up to the lightning.

The car was a five-year-old Plymouth Duster. It was empty. I listened and heard nothing but the wind. The lightning flashed again. In front of the car was a wide cleared space, maybe for parking. I saw no people. The rain smell was stronger now, and the thunder came closer upon the lightning. The storm was moving fast. I opened the car door and reached in and, crouched behind the open door, I turned on the head-lights.

Nothing happened. Nothing moved. I went flat on the ground, it was gravel, and looked underneath the car. Nothing. I got up carefully and moved out from the car in a crouch. The headlights made a wide theatrical swash of visibility in the darkness. Twenty feet in front of the car was Franco Montenegro's body and next to him was Candy's.

I went down on my knees beside her, but she was dead, and I knew it even before I felt for a pulse and couldn't find it. She had taken a couple of bullets in the body. There was blood all over her front. Beside her on the ground her purse was open. The .32 was out. Unfired. She'd tried. Like I'd told her to. There was a small neat hole in her forehead from which a small trickle of dark blood traced across her forehead. I glanced at Franco. He had a similar hole. The last two shots I'd heard. The coup de grace, one for each. I sat back on my heels and stared at Candy. Despite the blood and the bullet hole she looked like she had. For something as large as it is, death doesn't look like much at first.

The lightning and the thunder were nearly simultaneous now, and small spatters of rain mixed with the wind. I looked at Franco. Near his right hand was a gun. I moved over and, without touching the gun, lowered myself in a kind of push-up and smelled the muzzle. No smell of gunfire. He lay on his stomach, his face turned to one side. Blood soaked the back of his shirt. With my jaw clamped tight I rolled him over. There was no blood in front. The bullet hadn't gone through. He'd been shot from behind. Candy had been shot from in front. I got up and walked maybe fifteen feet back from Franco's body. On the soft gravel of the parking area were bright brass casings. The shooter had used an automatic, probably a nine-millimeter. I walked back and looked down at Candy. The rain was beginning to fall steadily, slanted by the wind. Already some of the blood was turning pink with dilution.

I looked around the parking area. There was noth-ing to see. I looked at Candy again. There was nothing more to see there either. Still, I looked at her. The rain was hard now, and dense, washing down on her upturned face. The wind was warm no longer. Candy didn't care. My clothing was soaked, my hair plastered flat against my skull. Rain running off my forehead blurred my vision. Candy's mascara had run, streak-ing her face. I stared down as the rain washed it away too.

"Some bodyguard," I said.

Chapter 26

I LEFT HER there in the rain with the headlights shining on her and walked back along the road to the fork and down the fork to my rented Ford. Brewster's car was gone. I was as wet as if I'd fallen overboard. I got in and sat in my wet clothes and started the engine. I pulled back onto Sepulveda and then up onto the Freeway and drove back toward Beverly Hills. The rain slashing across the headlights made silvery transluscent lines as it slanted past.

There wasn't much traffic. I made it back to Beverly Hills in fifteen minutes. At an all-night variety store I stopped and reported the murders. When they asked my name, I hung up and left. I ran the stop signs on Roxbury and drove up over the curb and onto Brewster's lawn. I left the doors open and the motor running as I rang his front doorbell. No one answered. I backed off two steps and kicked the door in. The whole frame splintered on my third kick and I went in. Nothing moved. No lights came on. I moved through the living room to the kitchen, then the dining room, then the den, and four more rooms that I couldn't name. No movement. I went up the front stairs two at a time and slammed in and out of rooms. Brewster wasn't there. In what must have been his bedroom was a vast circular bed. I picked up one end and turned it over to make sure he wasn't under it. He wasn't. I clattered down the stairs and out the back door toward the chauffeur's quarters. He wasn't there either. When I came out of the garage, I saw a red light flashing. The Bel-Air Patrol, on the job. I hadn't thought about the alarm system. I hadn't thought about much but Brewster.

I circled into the yard next door and walked down toward Roxbury Drive behind some shrubs. Lights went on in Brewster's house. I came out in the front yard next door to Brewster's house. A red and white private patrol car was parked near mine with the red light revolving on top. No one was in it. I walked past it to my car, got in, and drove away.

With the accelerator to the floor I headed for Century City. I parked on the street and went for Brewster's building on the run. It was still raining steadily. I hadn't put on my jacket, and the shoulder holster was clearly exposed. I was also soaking wet. People stared.

Brewster's building was locked. I looked at my watch. Ten fifteen. It would be locked. I went around to the other side. No luck. I went down one of the muddy lawns that slanted down from the plaza and tried the parking garage. It was locked, covered with one of those vertical iron grates that swing up when you operate a push button in your car. I had no push button. I could get in, but the only means available would risk the cops. I didn't want the cops. Yet.

I went back and sat in my rented car and thought. There was no reason to rush. Candy was in no hurry. I didn't even know if Brewster was in there. If he was, he'd have to come out sometime. If he wasn't he'd have to go in sometime. I could wait.

The rain was steady now; the wind that had brought it seemed to have died, but the rain was steady. It formed smooth, clear sheets as it ran down the windshield, and it made a steady, pleasant rattle on the roof of the car. Women coming from the restaurant, or the Century Plaza Hotel across the street, clutched skirts in tight against their legs as they crouched under umbrellas while their escorts stood manfully in the rain, often hatless, and hailed cabs. People moved hurriedly along, close to the buildings, as they always did in the rain, as if staying close to the artifice of civilization would ward off the elemental rain.

Trouble with waiting here for Brewster was that I didn't know which way he'd come in. But there was no place where I could locate myself where I would know. I'd just have to wait till they opened up in the morning and go in and take a look.

By midnight there was no one walking around anymore in the rain at Century City. At a quarter past midnight a police cruiser pulled up beside me and one of the cops said through his rolled-down window, "You got a problem, sir?"

I said, "Yeah, my car stalled and I think I flooded it. I'm letting it rest a couple minutes."

The cop said, "Okay. We'll swing by in a few minutes. If you can't start it, we'll get you someone."

I said, "Thank you, Officer."

The patrol car pulled away. But they'd be back, and if I was still there, it could be aggravation. Some cops are dumb and some aren't but none of them is naive. They'd be back to check my flooded-engine story.

I started up the Ford and rolled down onto Santa Monica. I went east a little ways and pulled into the parking lot behind the Beverly Hilton Hotel. I parked under a sign that said GUESTS ONLY, put on my Windbreaker, and walked back up Santa Monica to Century City. I was standing in the shadow of the entry to the Oceania Building when the cruiser came back, slowed down near where I'd parked, and then moved on.

The rain stayed with me all night. And even though it was Southern California summer, my teeth were beginning to chatter by the time the morning arrived. It came with a large gray light in the east but no visible sun, and the rain kept coming as if it always would. My clothes were damp against me and my eyes had the grainy feel of sleeplessness when the first of the day's workers began drifting in. Restaurant workers, early, bleary-eyed, collars up, white pants showing beneath rainwear. Then office workers, secretaries looking fresh-made and smelling of perfume, arrived in time to start the coffee, then at a successful hour, the executives, newly shaved, their London Fogs just back from the cleaners', their briefcases snapped tight against the weather—so their lunches wouldn't get wet. I didn't see Brewster.

At nine I left my doorway and found a phone booth and called Oceania. I got through to the woman in Brewster's outer office, the one who looked like Nina Foch.

"Pete in?" I said in a deep wealthy voice.

"No, sir. Mr. Brewster hasn't come into the office yet."

I laughed. "The old fox has been out prowling all night, I'll bet. When'll he be in?"

"I expect him at nine thirty, sir." Nina sounded a little disapproving.

"Well, when he comes in, tell him Ed's in town, and I'll call him later. Tell him I plan to whip his tail in racquetball as soon as he's ready."

"Yes, sir, I'll tell him," Nina said. Her disapproval was sharp now.

I hung up and went back to my spot in the doorway.

At nine forty-five I went into the Oceania Building, got in the elevator, and went up to Brewster's office at the top. Several people in the elevator looked at me covertly. I looked like a man who'd been standing around in the rain all night. I did not look like a man who should be on his way up to the executive floor. What they didn't know is that I never had.

Chapter 27

IN BREWSTER'S OUTER office there were three men in expensive suits sitting near their real leather briefcases. There was also one woman in an expensive business suit with a real leather briefcase and a real leather purse. I headed for the door to Brewster's office.

Nina Foch was quick as a weasel. "May I *help* you, sir?" she asked and stepped from her desk to put herself between me and the door. Her eyes widened as she remembered me. I put one hand against her near shoulder and swept her away backhand. I was pumped up as high as I can get and I put more force into it than I needed. She sprawled across her desk and onto the thick carpeted floor beyond it in a swirl of beige slip and panty hose.

I slammed Brewster's door open and headed on through the small library. Silhouetted against the gray light from his full-wall window, Brewster was at his desk. The library was set up for some kind of conference with an easel near the inner door. My shoulder banged it as I went by, and it went over, spilling its charts across the floor.

Simms was in the office with Brewster. He stepped in front of me as I came in, his hand going to his hip, under his coat. I hit him a left hook and a right cross and he went over backward, the half-drawn gun bouncing out of his hand and across the carpeting. Simms hit the couch, rolled half over, and landed on his right side on the floor. As I moved by him he grabbed at my ankle. I kicked loose of his hand and went for Brewster.

Brewster was out of his chair and around the other side of the desk, trying to keep it between me and him. His eyes were wide and his face was very pale. His tan looked yellow. I went over the desk after him the way you dive into surf and got hold of his coat with my left hand. He yanked back, and the struggle pulled me over the desk. I landed and came up the way you do out of a slide. Brewster pulled out of the jacket and headed for the outer office.

Simms was on his hands and knees going for the gun. As I went after Brewster he reached it. I stomped on his hand with my left foot and swung my right knee against the side of his head. He went over and down and didn't move. Brewster was through the library and into the outer office. I caught him at the door. I got a handful of his hair, yanked him back toward me, swung him past, and sent him sprawling back into the reception room. Two of the men had left. The businesswoman and the third man stood uncertainly. Nina Foch was on the phone. I yanked the cord out of the phone as I went by. Brewster was in a kind of crab-walk posture trying to scuttle one way or the other past me. The remaining businessman said, "Hey."

I ignored him. I got hold of Brewster by the shirt front and picked him up and pulled him up against me and then slammed him against the wall by the door to the library. Then I pulled him away and slammed him up against it again. His breath came out in loud grunts. The third businessman tried to grab me around the arms and pull me away. Without letting go of Brewster I said, "Get out of here. You don't know what you're into."

He tried to lock my arms down to my sides. Nina

Foch had run out the door. I let go of Brewster and broke the businessman's grip, and turned and hit him as hard as I could in the middle of his stomach. He said "Uff" and stepped back and doubled over and leaned against the door. Brewster tried to slip past me toward the door while that was happening, but I yanked him back and slammed him against the wall again. He pushed at my face with his hands. He wasn't very strong. Again against the wall. Then I stepped away. He sagged a little when I let him go. I slapped him open-handed across the face with my left hand, then with my right. Then left again. Then right. He put his hands up and covered his head. I punched him in the stomach. He gasped and dropped his hands. I slapped him left and right again. Each time I hit him, there was a pop inside me like red flashbulbs, and the muscles in my arms and shoulders and chest seemed to take energy from the action. If I closed my fists, I knew I'd kill him. He tried to cover his head and belly at the same time, but it was too much area, and my next slap was so hard, it knocked him over. He doubled up on the ground. His knees to his chest. His hands over his head. I kicked him in the kidneys. He wriggled over, trying to get away and keep me from his kidneys, and he bellied up for a moment. I stomped him in the stomach. Simms appeared in the doorway behind Brewster. His right eye was beginning to shut, and there was a trace of blood at the base of his nose. But he had the gun out, and he was squinting at me. The businesswoman, who had been watching all this time without a word, said, "Jesus Christ," and dove behind Nina's desk.

Simms was still groggy, and it made him slow. I stepped sideways and hacked the gun out of his hand. It hit the carpet near Brewster, and I scooped it up and stuck it in my hip pocket. As I straightened, Simms hit me a lunging, looping punch high on the head that jarred. I hit him twice with my left hand and one very hard right. He went back three steps. I went after him and knocked him backward into Brewster's office. He fell against Brewster's desk and slid down. I went back for Brewster. The businessman I had hit had some guts. He was still half doubled over but he hadn't left. He tried to grab my arm, and I threw him away from me. I reached down and brought Brewster back up against the wall again. Saliva drooled out of his mouth. His lip was cut and his nose was bleeding. I slapped him again.

Then something was behind me, and I hunched up and moved my head and something hit me hard on the top of my left shoulder. I let Brewster go and turned and saw a couple of Oceania security types in powder-blue uniforms. They had nightsticks. One of them had just hit me and was about to do it again. I caught his down-swinging right arm on my left forearm and hit him a right uppercut, and as he grunted and stepped back I slid my left hand along his arm and yanked the nightstick out of his hand. I hit him and then his buddy with the nightstick. One of them went down, the other one backed up, parrying with his stick. I hit him again, this time in the stomach and, when his guard came down, across the side of the head. He went down too. I grabbed hold of Brewster and pulled him up and walked him tippy-toe and backward into his private office and shut the door and locked it. I was seeing everything through a slightly reddish haze, but my head seemed as clear as mountain air, and all of the things that were happening seemed to have been happening at half speed, like a slow-motion movie, so that, despite the slight reddish haze, the whole sequence had gone forth with a wordless and almost stately clarity.

I took my gun out and pressed the barrel against

his upper lip directly under his nose where there was a slight indentation. He was wavering so, I had to hold his shirt with my left hand to keep him upright. I pressed the gun barrel harder against his upper lip.

My voice came out very softly, and it seemed very far from me. I said, "Here's what I think happened, Peter. I think you arranged to meet Franco out there in the oil field and you had Simms, and maybe somebody else, set up there early, and then you brought Candy out there and, being an efficient executive, you had Simms, and whoever, kill both of them on the spot. Two birds with one stone, you might say. That took care of anyone who seemed to threaten you. And then you came back and had a nice evening and a good sleep and came in here bright-eyed and bushy-tailed to greet another business day."

As I spoke he was trying to shake his head, but the pressure of the gun barrel under his nose made it hard, and so his head trembled laterally a bit. It was as close as he could come. To my right Simms was sitting up, his back against the couch.

"There'll be a hundred cops here in a minute, buddy," Simms said. His voice sounded slightly warped.

"The better to take you to the pokey, bright eyes," I said. "You burned Franco and the girl, didn't you?"

Simms just sat and looked at me.

"Didn't he?" I said to Brewster.

Brewster said "Un-uh" and tried again to shake his head. I banged him in the upper lip with the gun barrel.

"Didn't he?" I said.

"Un-uh."

I banged his upper lip again. Tears began to slide down his cheeks. "I followed you out there," I said. "I know you killed her. I won't mind shooting you right through your upper teeth. I liked her."

"Simms shot her," Brewster said. "He was just there to protect us from Franco, but he went crazy and shot her."

"How about that, Rollie," I said.

Simms looked at Brewster with disgust. "You got it right the first time," he said.

Someone tried the door to Brewster's office and then knocked. A voice said, "This is the police. Open the door."

I raised my voice. "If anyone comes in here, I'll blow both of these lizards apart."

There was silence. Then another voice said, "My name is Sergeant Eugene Hall. I'm going to call you on the phone in there, and we can talk. There's nothing we can't work out."

I said, "No. Not yet. I have a call to make. After that I'll talk with you. Call here in five minutes."

"Sure," Hall said. "No hurry. Just be easy."

I picked up the phone and got Information and called KNBS, and got John Frederics, the news director.

Chapter 28

WHEN I TOLD Frederics what I wanted, he said, "I'll come myself," and hung up. Maybe I had underrated him.

Brewster's lip was swelling, one eye was closing, blood still snuffled out of his nose. While I was talking, he had slid to the floor and now sat with his back against the window wall, his feet straight out in front of him. Simms had gone the other way. He was sitting on the couch now. There was a large bruise on his temple. He seemed to be missing a tooth. I noticed that there was a cut on the knuckles of my left hand.

Brewster said, "What are you going to do?" He had trouble speaking clearly.

I said, "You are going to confess on camera to the murder of Candy Sloan."

Brewster said, "What if I don't?"

I said, "I'll kill you."

"There's cops out there."

"Yeah, and how bad will they feel about you taking the jump when I tell them why?"

The phone rang. I picked it up and said, "Yeah?"

A voice said, "This is Gene Hall. What kind of a deal can we make?"

I said, "You know a homicide cop named Samuelson?"

Hall said, "Sure."

"Get him," I said. "Tell him I've got the people who killed Sam Felton, and Candy Sloan, and Franco

Montenegro. Tell him he can have them, but I want a little time to do something I have to do."

"Who you got in there? Secretary's so excited, I'm having trouble understanding her."

"I got Peter Brewster, who's the head of this company, and Rollie Simms, who's the chief of security."

"And what'd you say your name was?"

"Spenser."

"Okay. You want to stay by this phone so we can keep in touch?"

"Call anytime," I said and hung up.

Brewster and Simms sat as they had. I said to Brewster, "In a few minutes a guy from KNBS will be here with a cameraman. He's going to come in and interview you. You are going to give him a statement that I am going to type out for you right now."

I pulled an IBM Selectric typewriter over near me on its typing table, turned it on, and began to type with one finger while I held the gun toward Simms. Brewster had given up, but Simms was of sterner stuff.

The phone rang. I stopped typing and picked it up.

"Gene Hall again, Spenser. Guy from KNBS-TV out here says you wanted him to come in?"

"Yeah," I said. "Send him in."

"Well, there's a problem. You got two hostages now, I'd rather not add to the total."

"I don't blame you. I'll swap you one of mine. I'll send Simms out if you let the TV people in."

"That's still three for one," Hall said.

"Yeah. They tell you what we have in mind?"

"They told me what you told them."

"You been in touch with Samuelson yet?" I asked.

"Yeah. He's on his way."

"Okay. Why don't we sit tight until he gets here, then I'll talk with him."

"Okay by me, Spenser," Hall said. "Anything we can get you in the meantime?"

"Why do I think you guys will be less pleasant once I turn over Brewster and Simms?"

"Hey, no problem. You've been straight with us. We'll be straight with you. All we want is everything to go smooth. You want any coffee or anything?"

"No, thank you, Eugene," I said. I hung up and typed some more. In about three minutes the phone rang. I said, "Yeah?"

A voice, not Eugene's, said, "Spenser, what the fuck are you doing?"

"Samuelson?"

"Who'd you expect it to be, Barbara Walters?"

"One always has one's hopes," I said.

"What's going on?"

"You find Candy Sloan and Franco?"

"Yeah."

"Brewster and Simms shot them. Brewster's connected. Franco was trying to shake him down, and Candy was still trying to solve the thing. So Brewster put them both away at the same time."

"And you got Brewster in there?"

"Yes, and Simms. Simms probably pulled the trigger. Brewster wouldn't have the balls. But he called it."

"And you want the TV guys in there?"

"Yeah. You need an explanation?"

"No," Samuelson said. "I don't. Okay. We let them in, and I come too, and when it's over, you surrender them and you to me."

"You know why I want it this way," I said.

"Yes."

"Okay," I said. I hung up the phone. I took the typescript out of the typewriter. I handed it to Brewster. "When the TV people get set, you read that the way I wrote it. If you don't I'll shoot you six times."

"What's the difference," Brewster mumbled. "I read this, and the state will kill me."

"Not you," I said. "They haven't done away with

anyone out here in years. They probably have never done away with anyone as connected as you. You got all kinds of clout, Brewster. You could be back on the street in a few years. You can get into court and claim you were coerced. It might work. If you read that, you got lots of chances. If you don't, you have none. Look at me when I am speaking. *Look at me*. You know I'll do it."

Brewster stared at me with his eye and a half. He nodded. I walked over to the door and unlocked it and opened it up. I stayed out of the line of fire when I did. You can't tell when some SWAT cop will forget it's not television. Samuelson came in first, wearing his tinted glasses and looking relaxed. Frederics followed, not a hair out of place, gleaming and perfectly groomed. Behind him came a scruffy bearded black guy with a camera on his shoulder and a large shabby black bag hanging from a shoulder strap. Last came a young woman who was obviously having a scruff contest with the black man. She had equipment slung around over a man's shirt, jeans, and moccasins, and she carried a long pole with a microphone on it.

Samuelson went to the other side of the room and stood near Simms. Simms was looking at the floor. Frederics nodded at me.

I said to Brewster, "Get up." I had the gun held out full-length and shoulder level, pointed at him. A little drama doesn't hurt. Brewster got wearily to his feet. The black man muttered "Jesus" as he looked at Brewster's face.

Samuelson looked at me. "He was difficult to subdue," I said.

"I can tell," Samuelson said.

Frederics looked at his associates. "We ready?"

They both nodded. The soundwoman took the mike off its extender and handed it to Frederics. He looked at the camera. Then he said, "This is John Frederics.

I'm speaking to you from the offices of Oceania Industries at Century City, where an apparent hostage situation is in progress. The resolution of that situation requires that one of the hostages, Peter Brewster, the president of Oceania, read a statement. Mr. Brewster."

The cameraman moved the camera onto Brewster. Frederics held the mike in front of him. I kept the gun steady. Brewster was leaning against his desk, a little wobbly, but upright. He had my typescript in his hand. He read:

"A reporter from KNBS, Candy Sloan, through persistently good investigative reporting, finally uncovered the fact that I have been engaged in Mob-related criminal activity. She was about to report her story. To prevent that, I had her killed by a man named Rollie Simms. If it had not been for Candy Sloan, I would never have been caught."

There was silence. I brought the gun down, reversed it, and held it out, butt first, toward Samuelson. He reached around behind the soundwoman and took it and dropped it in his side pocket. Brewster simply stood where he was. Frederics brought the mike back to his own face, the camera shifted slightly.

"Right now in this room there is silence. A colleague is dead. This is John Frederics for KNBS News." He stood still for another moment, then made a safe sign with his hands. He looked at me for a moment. "It'll be on the air as soon as I get it back to the studio," he said.

I nodded. He nodded his head toward the door, and the three TV people left. The soundwoman was last and she looked back at me as she went. Her eyes were wet.

"Okay," Samuelson said. "Let's go downtown."

Chapter 29

IT WAS 11:03 P.M. in downtown Los Angeles. Since I'd come in about twelve hours ago with Samuelson, I had talked with three detectives, two assistant D.A.'s, a sheriff's investigator, a homicide captain, the chief of detectives (who called me "a bush-league fucking hot dog"), the department public relations officer, a guy from the mayor's office (who said something about "civic responsibility" that I didn't fully follow but seemed to be in substantial agreement with the chief of detectives), and a lawyer who KNBS had sent over to protect my constitutional rights, the same one they'd sent before. Now I was in Samuelson's office with the door closed, drinking maybe my eighty-third cup of really despicable black coffee and watching the late-night news with Samuelson on a nine-inch TV on top of a file cabinet in the left corner of the room.

On the screen Frederics, the news director, looking bigger and more natural, was sitting on the edge of a desk in what was obviously the KNBS newsroom, speaking directly into the camera.

"Every reporter covers stories of sudden death," he was saying. "But for all of us at KNBS News this has been a different story. This time the victim was one of us."

Samuelson was coatless, his tie was hanging unknotted, his shirt was unbuttoned, his sleeves rolled up above the elbows. He had his feet up on the corner of his desk as he watched, and he drummed with the fingers of his left hand softly on the desktop. I sipped some coffee. I didn't want it, but there wasn't anything else to do while I watched.

"KNBS feature reporter Candy Sloan was killed last night in the course of an investigation that linked motion picture industry figures to organized crime," Frederics said. I looked at myself in the dark window behind Samuelson's desk. My clothes had dried on me in complex wrinkles, my hair was stiff and angular. I had a two days' growth of beard, and I hadn't slept for a couple of days. I looked like a doorman at the drunk tank.

"Tinsel Town," I said. "Glamor."

Samuelson looked at me. "Land of dreams," he said. On the tube Frederics was summarizing the events that culminated in Candy's death.

"You ever notice that they never get it quite right," Samuelson said.

"Not even this one," I said.

"You want any more coffee?" Samuelson said.

"No." I felt a little sick from all that I'd drunk that day. I hadn't eaten in nearly as long as I hadn't slept. Samuelson got up and turned the sound down on the television so that Frederics was reduced to pantomime.

"You want to know what we got?" Samuelson said.

"Yeah."

"Okay. We got lucky. Brewster couldn't wait to blame Simms for everything. We read him his rights and warned him about using what he said and told him he needn't talk without his lawyer, but he was in such a goddamn sweat to get it on record that Simms was the one who did everything, that he just kept right on bleating, and Simms got mad and started replying, and we got about everything they had. They might have been a little punchy from having been forcibly apprehended."

I nodded.

"Anyway," Samuelson said, "we got the files out on Simms, and he's got a yellow sheet, looks like it belongs to Attila the Hun. He's a Mob enforcer. Brewster's tied into the Mob and that means they're tied into him. They put Simms into Oceania to keep an eye on things."

"Can you use what you got in court?" I said.

Samuelson shrugged. "Ain't my department. D.A.'s guys say maybe. But you know how it goes. There's going to be expensive lawyers defending Brewster. They'll say he was coerced by you. They'll say he was not competent when he spoke without a lawyer. They'll mention the fundamental concepts of American justice. Our side will be argued by some kid two years out of U.S.C." Samuelson shrugged again.

"Start earlier," I said. "Why did Franco kill Felton?"

"Franco was a collector. Most recently for Ray Zifkind. About five, six years ago, Summit Studios was going down the chute, and Ray Zifkind bailed them out. That put the head of Summit, guy named Hammond, in the Mob's pocket."

"I know Hammond," I said. "Zifkind the stud duck out here?"

"Yeah. Anyway, one thing led to another, Brewster got in on it. The way you might if you were playing cards and caught a guy cheating. Instead of blowing the whistle, you play along with him. Let him make you money too. You ever play cards?"

"Yeah. I get the idea."

"Pretty soon Summit Pictures and Oceania products were getting the edge in the marketplace, and Zifkind was making dough and Brewster was making dough, and Summit was making dough. Now and then some theater owner in Omaha would get roughed up, or a lumber wholesaler in Olympia, Washington, would have his warehouse burned, but that's business, and everything seemed jake to everybody—except maybe the lumber wholesaler or the movie theater guy in Omaha—until Candy Sloan comes along."

On the silent TV screen Frederics had stopped speaking. The camera zoomed back and held for a long shot of the whole newsroom, then the screen went gray. I got up and turned it off.

Samuelson kept on talking. "Some of this I picked up here and there—we been looking into this for a while ourselves. We picked Hammond up this afternoon—some of this I got from the two crooners downstairs. She talks to Felton, and Felton gets nervous and tells Hammond, and Hammond bucks it along to Brewster, and so forth, and eventually Franco Montenegro gets sent out to slap Sloan around a little and scare her off. They don't want to burn a reporter if they can help it."

"I still don't know why Franco burned Felton."

"Patience," Samuelson said. "I'm getting to that. What me and you don't know is that Felton has been the conduit for profits from Summit to Zifkind. And what nobody knows, including Brewster and Hammond and Zifkind, is that Felton is skimming. But Franco knew."

If I'd been a cartoon character, a light bulb would have appeared in a balloon above my head. "And Franco cut himself a piece," I said.

"Smart," Samuelson said. "Smart eastern dude. You go to Haavahd?"

"I have a friend who's taking a course there," I said.

"Must rub off," Samuelson said. Through the clear glass door of his office I could see a wall clock in the squad room. It said eleven thirty-eight. "So Felton and Franco are nibbling some vigorish of their own off the Mob's vig. And nobody knows this."

"And when we got so close to Felton that he was

— 179 —

sure to take the fall, Franco had to kill him," I said.
" 'Cause if the Mob found out what they were doing,
it—"

Samuelson nodded. "Yes," he said, "slow, painful
and certain. The part I like is that Felton puts in a
call to Franco to come bail him out and of course
invited in his own killer."

"Franco was right," I said. "Felton didn't have the
stuff. He'd have told everything he knew to everybody
who asked him about thirty seconds after you got him
in here."

"The thing is that what Sloan's boyfriend—what's
his name?"

"Rafferty," I said, "Mickey Rafferty. But he wasn't
her boyfriend."

"What Rafferty saw when Felton gave Franco some
dough wasn't what they and you and me thought it
was. It was just Franco's private little gig with Felton.
But it got the whole thing rolling, and it got Hammond scared and Brewster and, I suppose, eventually
Ray Zifkind, but we'll never get close to him."

"And Brewster," I said. I felt as if I would never
leave the chair I was in. As if I were slowly fossilizing,
the living part of me dwindling deeper and deeper
inside. All my energy was focused on listening to Samuelson. "Franco try to shake him down?"

"Yep. Needed the dough, I suppose, to get out of
here and away from Zifkind and us."

"And Brewster figured Candy was getting too close?"
I said.

"Yeah. He didn't believe she was as taken with him
as she acted."

"So he got Simms, and maybe somebody else—anybody else?"

"Yeah, soldier named Little Joe Turcotte. We're
looking around for him now."

"So he got Simms and Little Joe to go out early and

wait for Franco, and when Franco showed up, they gunned him. One of them used an automatic."

"Turcotte," Samuelson said.

"And they killed both of them while I was wandering around in the oil field."

"Don't make you happy, I guess," Samuelson said.

"Nope. I haven't been right since I got here."

"Can't see how you could have done much better," Samuelson said.

I didn't say anything.

"She was going to keep at it," Samuelson said. "No way you could have kept her from it."

"The thing is," I said. My voice didn't seem to be very closely connected to me. I paused and tried to think what I wanted to say. "The thing is," I said, "that she did what she did because she didn't want to be just another pretty face in the newsroom, you know. Just a broad that they used to dress up the broadcast. She wanted to prove something about herself and about being a woman, I guess, and what got her killed—when you come down to it—was, she thought she could use being female on Brewster. When it came down to it, she depended on—" I stopped again. I couldn't think of the right phrase.

"Feminine wiles," Samuelson said.

"Yeah," I said. "Feminine wiles. And it got her killed."

Chapter 30

THE PHONE RANG on Samuelson's desk. The clock in the squad room said twelve twenty-five. I sat almost insentient while Samuelson listened to the phone. He said "Mmm" two, maybe three times, then listened some more. Then hung up without saying anything else.

"D.A.'s office wants to prosecute you," Samuelson said.

I nodded.

"Charges include resisting arrest, assault and battery on the Oceania security people, and being a bush-league fucking hot dog."

"They been talking to your chief of detectives," I said.

"They were toying with a kidnapping charge, but since the two guys you held were murder suspects, they don't think it will stand up. But they also got some new hostage laws they want to try out, and they'll probably charge you under one of them."

"Good chance for them to practice," I said.

"Yeah."

We were quiet. The squad room behind us was nearly empty. Samuelson rubbed the back of his neck with his right hand.

"They want me to bring you down and book you."

The air conditioner under the window behind Samuelson cycled on with a small thump and a sound of air blowing.

"You got an airline ticket?" Samuelson said.

"In my wallet."

"Okay," he said. "Let's go."

We went out of his office. He shut off the lights and closed the door carefully behind him. We walked through the squad room and out of the corridor and took the elevator down to the first floor.

"This way," Samuelson said.

We walked out the front door and down the steps. The rain had stopped but the dampness still hung in the air. The night was hot and steamy. And you knew it would rain again soon. We walked around the corner and got into an unmarked Chevy sedan. Samuelson drove. We went onto the Harbor Freeway and headed south.

I had my head back against the seat, almost asleep. "You going to book me in Long Beach?" I asked.

"No."

We turned off the Harbor Freeway at the Santa Monica Freeway and went west.

There was no traffic and Samuelson drove fast. In a few minutes we were in West L.A. We turned off the Santa Monica and onto the San Diego Freeway around a big involute cloverleaf. We went south toward the airport.

It was ten of one when Samuelson headed down Century Boulevard toward the L.A. airport.

"What airline you got a ticket for?" he said.

"American."

The airport was brilliantly lighted, the lighting making an orange-yellow blur in the mist that seemed to hover over it about twenty feet up. It had the feel of a bright emptiness that a shopping mall has after hours. A single yellow cab rolled past us, going toward L.A. Two airline types in uniform waited at a bus stop in front of the international terminal.

Samuelson parked in front of American and we went

in. There was a flight at 1:20 for Dallas/Fort Worth that connected for Boston. It was boarding at Gate 46. Samuelson showed his badge to the cop at the security check, and they didn't make a fuss when the metal detector buzzed at Samuelson's gun. Mine was back somewhere in a drawer at the homicide bureau.

At Gate 46 Samuelson said to me, "Get on. Go to Boston. When it's time to testify, I want you back."

"I thought you were supposed to book me," I said.

"You escaped as I was bringing you down," Samuelson said.

"This won't get you promoted to captain," I said.

"I flunked the captain's exam twice already," Samuelson said. "Just be sure to come back when it's time to testify."

"I'll come back," I said.

"Yeah," Samuelson said. "I know."

I was swaying slightly as we stood there. It was one fifteen. I put out my hand. Samuelson shook it.

"You did what you could for that broad, Spenser," Samuelson said. "Including what you did at Oceania afterward."

I nodded.

"D.A. don't understand that," Samuelson said. "Neither does the chief."

I nodded again.

Samuelson said, "Nobody's perfect."

"That's for goddamn certain," I said.

I was asleep in my seat before we took off. Except for a half-conscious plane change in Dallas I slept straight through to Boston and dreamed of Susan Silverman all the way home.

MORE ABOUT PENGUINS, PELICANS
AND PUFFINS

For further information about books available from Penguins please write to Dept EP, Penguin Books Ltd, Harmondsworth, Middlesex UB7 0DA.

In the U.S.A.: For a complete list of books available from Penguins in the United States write to Dept DG, Penguin Books, 299 Murray Hill Parkway East Rutherford, New Jersey 07073.

In Canada: For a complete list of books available from Penguins in Canada write to Penguin Books Canada Ltd, 2801 John Street, Markham, Ontario L3R 1B4.

In Australia: For a complete list of books available from Penguins in Australia write to the Marketing Department, Penguin Books Australia Ltd. P.O. Box 257, Ringwood, Victoria 3134.

In New Zealand: For a complete list of books available from Penguins in New Zealand write to the Marketing Department, Penguin Books (N.Z.) Ltd. P.O. Box 4019, Auckland 10.

In India: For a complete list of books available from Penguins in India write to Penguin Overseas Ltd. 706 Eros Apartments, 56 Nehru Place, New Delhi 110019.